OLIVER NOCTURNE

Catch Up on the Rest of the Series:

OLIVER NOCTURNE

THE VAMPIRE'S PHOTOGRAPH

Oliver meets Emalie and Dean. Together they uncover the mystery of Oliver's destiny, but their friendship comes at a tragic price.

THE SUNLIGHT SLAYINGS

Dean returns as a zombie with a mysterious master. Oliver and Dean race to figure out who's really behind a series of vampire slayings that are being blamed on Emalie and her growing power.

BLOOD TIES

During a harrowing "vacation" into the vampire underworld of Morosia, the terrible truth of Oliver's prophecy is revealed, as well as the identity of Dean's powerful master.

THE DEMON HUNTER

A gruesome series of murders are being blamed on Oliver's brother Bane. As the gang tries to clear his name, they uncover shocking truths about Oliver's approaching destiny.

THE ETERNAL TOMB

The Darkling Ball approaches and with it the Anointment which will seal Oliver to his fate. Oliver, Emalie and Dean must use all their powers as they try to save the world before it's too late.

OLIVER NOCTURNE

the Triad of Finity

KEVIN EMERSON

COREY'S ROOM PRESS
SEATTLE, WA

Oliver Nocturne
The Triad of Finity
ISBN 13: 9780615472096
ISBN 10: 0-615-47209-5

Copyright © 2011 by Kevin Emerson
Cover Art and Design by Carl Nelson
Interior Layout and Design by Martha Brockenbrough

Printed in USA by Alphagraphics of Seattle
Printed on Finest Yet Offset 100% Recycled Post-Consumer Weight Stock,
FSC Certified

All Rights Reserved. Published by Corey's Room Press, Seattle, WA.
First Edition, April 2011

This book is dedicated to the readers who commented tirelessly on my message board or emailed me demanding a sixth book. Without your enthusiasm and support, I'm not sure this would have happened.

And to M.W. and M.B., whose belief in these books never wavered.

AUTHOR'S NOTE

Almost four years ago, I was sitting in my backyard on a sunny Seattle afternoon reading a draft of the first Oliver Nocturne book when I was struck by an idea. I started writing a scene in pen on the title page, a scene that I felt certain was how Oliver's story should end. It was a big idea, something I'd never considered before, and it changed the scope and trajectory of the entire series.

Everything I did after that was crafted with that ending in mind, yet I didn't really know how I was going to get there. Scholastic wanted five books, and there was no guarantee of more after that. Still, as I worked through the story, I realized that to set up that ending just right, I wouldn't be able to get there by the end of Book 5: *The Eternal Tomb*.

As I wrapped up that book, I knew I'd need to write more, but how long would the series need to be? For awhile I had a plan to write a few more volumes, and you may notice a moment in this book where one of the characters mentions a whole potential novel I'd been thinking of, but in the end, I realized that one more book would do the trick. And technically, this book is a bit longer than the others, so I guess 6.25 books is the final answer.

Anyway, what really matters is that when you get to the last pages of the last chapter of this book (just before the Epilogue), you will find that old, hand-scrawled ending, now neatly typed but nearly word-for-word. When you create something, all you can really ask for is to finish it the way you wanted, and to walk away from it knowing you were true to your vision and your heart. I feel that way about Oliver Nocturne.

I hope you enjoy Oliver's final journey... to the Gate, and his destiny.

— Kevin Emerson, March 2011

PREVIOUSLY ON OLIVER NOCTURNE....

Oliver felt like a bolt of lightning had struck him in the chest, only it stayed impaled there, and as Emalie pulled away, turning her tear-streaked face and starting down the roof, Oliver felt like the bolt was being ripped back out of him, each sharp edge tearing him open further, making a wound that would never heal. *Don't... go....*

Emalie flashed a final smile in their direction, and winked out of sight.

"Bye," said Oliver weakly.

There was no reply in the night.

CONTENTS

PROLOGUE

At the center of everything stood a Gate.

The Gate had never been opened. It had been made, and then shut. Some said that the sound of its closing began the universe. And ever since then, it stood watch over the airless, blood red plains of Nexia. Above, stars and planets hung like crystal ornaments in a pure black sky. Nebulae and galaxies fluttered and shimmered. Rings of dust and star fire arced and spun. Wormholes spiraled in inky swirls out to the wide universe beyond.

The Gate stood among the ruins of an ancient civilization: broken amethyst spires, jade columns, enormous statue heads with blank expressions and solid gold eyes, all stuck in the crimson rock as if it had solidified around them. The Architects had once lived here, and there was much debate about who they really were, and what they really wanted.

But as to what they had done, most beings who were *in-the-know* understood: The Architects had built the

<I>

universe, then the Gate. When they were finished, each had taken up a sentry position in one of the worlds. They were guardians of their creations. Watchers. All except one, and she, much to the displeasure of her brothers and sisters, had been very busy.

This Architect had taken a most dangerous assignment, watching over the world of Earth, where the effects of Finity were most severe. Finity was time with an end. In the matter-based worlds like Earth, things formed and unformed, lived and died, all ruled by time. It was a maddening state of existence for any creature, knowing that their time would someday run out. It was especially maddening for any being whose existence had formerly been *in*finite.

This was the case with the Architect, Desiree. Though Finity wasn't going to snuff her out, it had warped her otherwise far-reaching mind and made it prone to Finity's poles: light and dark, which created the intense qualities of good and evil on Earth. The rest of the Architects had known this was a danger, but so was everything else in the universe. And besides, Desiree had asked for the job, actually competed for it, because—and it would shock the many higher beings of the universe to hear this—*life* was the Architects' most prized creation.

But Desiree was not the only being on Earth who was suffering due to Finity. There was another group, demons of the higher worlds who had been sentenced for their crimes to Earth as the ultimate form of universal punishment. They'd been put inside mortal bodies and

<2>

doomed to die as dust within just a few short centuries. These pitiable beings were known on Earth as vampires, and they did not like their lot in the universe one bit.

And so they were planning to escape. To open the Gate and restart the universe, to be eternal once more, to be free. That opening the Gate would cause a great upheaval sure to reshuffle the entire order of the universe, not to mention kill all the living beings, was of little concern. Anything was better than being trapped in the eternal tomb of Earth.

The Gate didn't care about the yearnings of the *vampyr* or the manipulations of Desiree, nor even about the price of happy thoughts on the Merchynt market or any of the other business of the many worlds. All it cared about was its function. There was a great debate about whether or not the Gate was meant to be opened or to remain closed, but the Gate knew exactly what it had been made to do. And it knew that this purpose was soon to be tested, and that this test involved the ancient demon who was now before it.

He's late, said the Gate.

The gentleman Illisius, an ancient and powerful demon whose features seemed ageless, sat cross-legged in the middle of a road made of black obsidian shards. He pushed up the cuff of his fine pinstriped suit and checked the seven dials of his silver watch. *Somewhat,* he replied.

Perhaps your plan is in jeopardy.

Illisius smiled. *On the contrary. Our plan is nearing its completion. You sensed the Anointment, did you not?*

<3>

Indeed. Yet it did not go as you expected.

That would be true, if we were foolish enough to believe in expectations. We cannot know what will happen until it happens. Therefore, the fact that the Anointment happened means it was a success.

The Gate sighed. *Yes, but there were complications.*

Illisius smiled. *One being's complications are another being's opportunities.*

I suppose, said the Gate.

Two years passed.

Then a sound broke the total silence. Beeping. Illisius once again consulted his watch. *Ah, yes.* He stood, brushed off his pants, and picked up his briefcase. It was made of iridescent, scaled skin, and refracted prisms of the golden Gate light.

Going somewhere? The Gate asked.

As if in reply, hooves crunched against the road. Illisius turned to see the distant form of a coach, pulled by two zombie horses, clattering near.

I thought you were waiting for the vampire boy, said the Gate.

I was.

The stagecoach door opened. A pale hand retreated back into the coach, belonging to a figure sitting in the shadows.

The Gate considered this figure. *Interesting.*

Isn't it? said Illisius. He turned, a broad smile revealing his bright, blade-edged teeth. His ancient eyes, the color of battle-scarred bronze, gleamed. *Like I said,*

<4>

things happen. He started toward the coach. *Seems I'll be making a house call, instead. And when we return, we shall open you.*

Bold words, from someone who said we can't know the future, said the Gate.

Illisius laughed. *True,* he said, *but all the same... we shall. See you soon.*

<5>

<6>

Chapter 1

THE MENTEUR'S HEART

Night falls pleasantly early in Seattle in November. The days are brief, cloudy, barely ever seeming brighter than twilight. On the rare afternoons when the sun even appears, it cowers in the far corner of the sky, pale, fleeting. The mountains gather their first blankets of snow; the ocean cools to gray; the last leaves fall. Humans wrap themselves tightly in coats and scarves. They retreat into their homes earlier, huddling in the warmth and light to celebrate their harvest. And beyond their closed window shades, the city's other inhabitants enjoy the long, dark hours.

This November had been exceptionally rainy, and that put a spring in the lurking steps of all who woke at dusk, with the notable exception of a certain vampire family, who rose one Thursday evening with a foreboding event on their calendar.

Mr. Crevlyn was scheduled to arrive promptly at eight.

<7>

"This sucks," said Oliver Nocturne as he entered the kitchen and slouched down on a stool at the center island.

"Now, now," said Phlox from across the kitchen, where she worked over the gleaming titanium forge, her back to him. "It will be fine."

Oliver dropped his heavy backpack to the polished stone floor with a thud and leaned on his elbows. He brushed his hair from his eyes—he'd been letting it grow the last few months, and had even put a green streak in the front— and took a sip from the lead goblet before him. He was glad for the sweet, slightly citrusy taste of kangaroo blood. It was one of his favorites. Still, it wasn't enough to change his current mood. "It's not going to be fine," he muttered.

"Well," said Phlox, turning around with a steaming skillet in one hand and a spatula in the other, "there's nothing we can do except endure it." She was dressed smartly as usual, her platinum hair wrapped up in a severe bun.

Oliver rolled his eyes. How many times had Phlox said that lately? "Why do we have to endure it? How about we tell them *no*, for once, and then—"

Phlox's eyes flared from their usual hazel to a brilliant turquoise. "Charles," she began— but stopped.

Oliver looked away. It rarely happened anymore, but sometimes, when she was flustered, Phlox still slipped. Oliver didn't feel mad at his mom for this. Instead, he felt a surge of... weird. It only happened when he was acting defiant or insolent, like his older brother Bane used to,

<8>

before he'd been slain to dust. Actually, Oliver was maybe proud of that, of being able to channel his brother now and then. Except it made him miss Bane, too. Right about now, Bane would have come sauntering up the stairs, probably slapped Oliver on the back of the head before dropping down beside him.... Instead, the kitchen was silent.

"Sorry," said Phlox quietly. She slid a trio of deep fried dumplings onto a cast iron plate. "Oliver," she began again, "you have to understand...." Her eyes, no longer glowing, arched toward the ceiling. This was Phlox's now well-understood reminder that everything they said was being monitored by hidden microphones.

Oliver sighed. "I know," he said dejectedly, "but, sometimes I just...." He shook his head. "Whatever." He reached for the plate and Phlox's delicate ivory hand fell atop his. He felt the reassuring cool of her skin, the razor scratch of her burgundy-painted fingernails.

"It will be okay," she said.

Oliver nodded, but that was getting harder to believe. He slid the plate over and took a bite of a still-sizzling fritter, his taste buds delighting, in spite of his mood, at the burst of molten chocolate inside, spiced with habañero concentrate and especially sweet with the addition of extracted lynx adrenaline, which not only tasted like mint but was known to have relaxing properties. Like the kangaroo blood, this was another rare treat that Phlox surely intended to counteract the ordeal Oliver was about to endure.

<9>

Footsteps clicked up the stone staircase and Sebastian swept into the kitchen. "Hey Ollie," he said, rubbing Oliver's hair as he passed. He was dressed in a sleek black suit. He picked up a goblet at the far end of the island, took a long swig, then traded it for a stone mug of coffee which had been sitting on a small warming plate on the counter, bubbling away. Vampires liked their coffee hot, preferably boiling. He tapped a dash of cayenne pepper into it before drinking.

"Any updates about our guest?" Phlox asked as she opened the refrigerator. Its silver door rose upward to the ceiling with a hiss.

"Nothing new," said Sebastian, "Same as the other visits, as far as I've been told."

"You know," said Phlox thinly as she arranged the clear plastic bags of blood hanging on racks in the fridge, "Mother told me that Mr. Crevlyn's not even technically a physician anymore. Apparently he was formally stripped of his license for *questionable* practices. That's why he took the job at the Asylum Colony. They have looser standards." Oliver's grandparents lived in Morosia, the underworld beneath Europe.

"Sounds like the perfect person to be the new head of Half-Light," said Sebastian grimly.

Phlox turned to him and her mouth curled skeptically.

"What did he do, anyway?" Oliver asked. "To lose his license?"

"Well," Phlox began, "it's all confidential, but Mother says the word in Morosia is that at the Asylum Colony,

<10>

Mr. Crevlyn was in charge of the demosapien alchemy division."

"What's that?"

"The mixing of demons with living humans," said Sebastian gruffly, checking his watch, "and it's nothing we need to discuss further."

Oliver was fine with ending the talk. Humans and demons.... It reminded him of something he didn't want to think about, anyway: The *other* thing he had to do before school tonight.

"Or maybe we should be asking someone," Phlox began, and she raised her head so that the listening devices would hear her loud and clear, "whether it's appropriate for our son to be in the company of someone with that kind of background."

Sebastian looked at her and shrugged, a gesture of powerlessness that Oliver hated to see. Mr. Crevlyn was the new head of operations at the powerful Half-Light consortium, Sebastian's employer, and he'd personally put himself in charge of examining Oliver, to determine his "mental state."

Oliver understood why: He was, after all, the key figure in Half-Light's plot to open the Nexia Gate, thereby freeing all the vampires from Earth and remaking the universe, which, as a consequence, would also destroy Earth and everything in it. Half-Light had been planning this for decades, maybe even centuries, according to a prophecy which stated that a sired but demonless vampire child could open the Gate. Oliver was that child. And now

<11>

that the Anointment had been completed, there was no turning back. Only, it was more complicated than that, for a number of reasons, but mainly because of... *don't think about*— Oliver tried to warn himself, but a strong and painful memory arrived anyway:

Emalie.

Oliver felt a moment of fuzziness, like a wave had washed over his mind. He was brought back to his senses by a thudding knock on the sewer door downstairs.

"That's him," said Sebastian. He headed for the stairs, his lips pursed.

Oliver stuffed the troubling thoughts away. He needed to focus to make it through what was about to happen. He finished his fritters and listened as the door opened, greetings were exchanged, and footsteps returned to the kitchen.

Sebastian entered first. "Mr. Crevlyn is here."

He strolled in wearing a bright grin, the kind that was too wide, as if it had been practiced often. He wasn't much older than Phlox and Sebastian—Oliver would have guessed about three hundred—but was uncharacteristically wide and soft around the middle for a vampire. And that was the oddity of his face, too: its breadth, its tendency to shine too brightly around those gleaming, peach-colored irises, without care for the other sources of light in its sphere. Neither Mr. Crevlyn's suit—a dour, mulch-colored tweed—nor his accessories—conservatively striped tie, modest watch and briefcase—gave away his true nature, but his smiling face revealed a disquieting confidence, that self-assured comfort in oneself that seemed to be most apparent in the most dangerous figures.

"Good evening, Nocturnes," said Mr. Crevlyn smoothly.

He stepped into the kitchen and moved aside. There was a sound of shuffling metal and another figure entered. The crimson-robed form had to hunch to fit into the kitchen. Its shackled wrists and ankles jangled. Its face was hidden by a hood. A Codex, from Half-Light's private library.

"And how are we tonight, Oliver?" Mr. Crevlyn asked. The smile widened, the cheeks contorting, creating extra folds.

Oliver looked away. "Fine."

"Well then, shall we?" He looked to Phlox. "Coffee would be lovely," he said, as if she'd offered. "Spiked, if you don't mind."

Phlox nodded slightly, her mouth a thin, tight line. "Of course."

Oliver slumped off the stool and headed for the living room, where he dropped onto one of the leather couches. Phlox and Sebastian sat on the other, to his left. Mr. Crevlyn spread himself on the edge of a high backed chair across from him.

The Codex lowered to the floor, sitting cross-legged on a pillow. Its black, skeletal hands produced a small mortar made of flecked stone. There was a pinch of dried brown incense in the bowl. The Codex struck a match and lit it. A thin trail of gray smoke slithered up into the room.

<13>

Mr. Crevlyn flipped open his briefcase and removed a bundle of black velvet. He placed this on the table and unwrapped it, revealing a long, pink crystal shard. "*Veritesssch*," he whispered, and the crystal began to glow. Oliver knew it well enough: a Menteur's Heart, similar to a human lie detector, though quite a bit more powerful and accurate, as demons and vampires were much more skilled at deception than a creature with a soul could ever be.

Oliver felt like the Heart was barely necessary in his case. He didn't bother lying anymore. It never worked out.

"Well now," said Mr. Crevlyn. He looked at Oliver, eyes bright. "How are we feeling these days?"

"Fine," muttered Oliver.

"And how is school?"

"Okay."

"Good," said Mr. Crevlyn. "All right, then: Just for the sake of clarity, let's review: If I'm correct, this all began when you met the Orani girl. She invaded your home, and yet due to your Human Sympathizing Syndrome— an unfortunate consequence of your sired origins that we know is not your fault—you let her live and befriended her."

Oliver just stared ahead but inside he rolled his eyes. This was all ridiculous. *This all began*, he thought, *when I was stolen from my human parents and sired*, but he didn't blame Phlox and Sebastian for that. They had merely wanted a child, and hadn't been able to have one. So they'd volunteered to raise the prophecy children. Oliver's origins were really Half-Light's doing. And because of those origins, he'd felt strange his entire existence. But that wasn't why he'd befriended Emalie. It had been because she was actually interested in him, not to mention how she was interesting herself, fascinating even... *Gone*....

"Then," Mr. Crevlyn continued, "there was the mix-up with the murder of the Orani girl's cousin and whether the subsequent zombie was your minion—"

"His name is Dean," Oliver added. He hated how Mr. Crevlyn always did this: not using names as if they somehow weren't worthy.

Mr. Crevlyn paused for only a moment, his smile undiminished. "Of course it is. And all of that business was, in fact, orchestrated by the LeRoux girl—"

"Lythia," Oliver added.

"Yes, she was the zombie's true master, and she was trying to steal your prophecy. So, again, not your fault." Mr. Crevlyn nodded like Oliver was supposed to feel good about that. "Then, let's seen, following that we had the brief period where the girl tried to slay you—"

"Which wasn't *Emalie's* fault," Oliver interrupted. He felt his anger growing. Mr. Crevlyn's smile lessened. Phlox eyed Oliver severely, but kept silent as he continued. "She was being controlled by The Brotherhood of the Fallen. *They* were the ones who wanted to slay me."

"Indeed," said Mr. Crevlyn. "And finally, there was the continual misinformation given to you by the rogue Architect. Her deceptions led you to seek out Selene, the Orani oracle, to search for your original human parents,

<15>

and to try to thwart your Anointment. Again, Desiree is a powerful being, and so one can hardly blame you for all that, can they?" Mr. Crevlyn's smile returned.

"Sure," said Oliver. He knew by now that this was one of the goals of Mr. Crevlyn's visits: to make Oliver feel good about himself and his destiny. And an obvious second goal was to reform Oliver's image, and by extension his parents' image, in the Half-Light vampire community. There was much suspicion and mistrust as to whether the Nocturnes could handle being the family of the Nexia prophecy, but now that the Anointment had succeeded, and there was no other choice, Half-Light wanted to make sure that everyone saw the Nocturnes in a good light. It wasn't for Oliver and his family, it was for the safety of the prophecy, just like everything had always been.

Sebastian spoke up. "And has Half-Light determined the whereabouts of Dead Desiree?"

"She remains... unaccounted for," said Mr. Crevlyn with a sigh, his smile faltering only momentarily, "but all measures are being taken to find her." He turned back to Oliver. "Well, I must say, Oliver, it is a testament to your strength and guile that you are still here and not a pile of dust, considering all the danger you've been exposed to! This alone should prove your worth as the chosen vampire, don't you think?"

Oliver just shrugged. "Sure."

"The closest he came to dust was when Half-Light tried to slay him," said Phlox thinly.

"Ah yes," said Mr. Crevlyn, "well, these things do

<16>

happen. Luckily, as the new Director, I can assure you that I have a far better handle on things."

Mr. Crevlyn reached out and ran his hand over the Menteur's Heart. Its glow brightened, flickering on all of their faces. He was increasing its sensitivity for this final question. "Now then, we really just have our one last usual piece of business to attend to before we're finished for the evening." He leaned forward. "Oliver: Do you, or does anyone you know, have any idea as to the current whereabouts of the Orani girl?"

Oliver felt Phlox and Sebastian's eyes on him. He felt a rush of nerves in his gut. The crystal's glow made spots in his vision. At full strength, it would detect even the slightest hint of a lie...

But, unfortunately, Oliver only had the truth to tell. "No."

Mr. Crevlyn gazed at the crystal, and when its glow did not waver, his brow almost seemed to furrow. "And if she does try to contact you, or alert you to her whereabouts, I can only urge you, again, to let us know."

Oliver nodded. "Sure."

Mr. Crevlyn leaned over, blew out the crystal, and wrapped it up. The Codex's eyes extinguished. Both stood. "Oliver, on behalf of the Half-Light Consortium, I want to thank you and your family for your continued cooperation."

"As if we had a choice," growled Sebastian.

Mr. Crevlyn shrugged his eyebrows and continued. "We'll see you next time. And in the meantime, rest

<17>

assured: we will be watching out for your best interests. Now, we don't want you to be late for school."

Oliver just glared at him.

"You can let yourself out," said Sebastian.

"Certainly," Mr. Crevlyn replied, his grin unfaltering.

Oliver still hadn't moved as the sewer door clicked shut. Phlox leaned over and stroked his arm. "You did great. We endure these things, and we move on."

Oliver didn't reply. He felt blank.

"You should get to school," said Sebastian. "I'll walk there with you, if you—"

"Nah." Oliver got to his feet. "It's fine. I'm… fine." He wasn't, not at all, but he still had that thing to do before school and now he felt like he needed to more than ever.

Oliver headed into the kitchen, grabbed his bag and hurried out.

<18>

Chapter 2

EMPTY SPACES

Oliver emerged from the sewers and trudged through the falling evening to school. He was early; the last humans were still loitering out front, hunched against the drizzle, waiting for rides. Oliver walked right by, continuing up the street and across a damp park.

He knew that right now, in some Half Light office downtown, his ankle sensor was announcing that he'd left his prescribed route to school, and an occupied vampire sentry was no doubt being dispatched to follow his movements, likely in the form of a bat or owl. But if he hurried, he should have enough time....

He leapt easily onto the roof of a city bus then sat, sweatshirt hood over his head, remembering a time when it had been hard for him to perform what now seemed like the most basic work controlling the forces. The first time he'd leapt onto this bus, he'd almost fallen off the side, and barely avoided being noticed.

<19>

Ten blocks later, he stood and vaulted off, over the streetlights, landing cat-like atop a house. He continued roof-to-roof. Some of the yards below had already been strung with holiday lights, splashes of warmth among bare, dripping branches. Their cheery glow only made the crowding sense of memory thicker in Oliver's mind.

He hopped one last time, landing on a triangular peak, and looked down. This yard was dark, consumed by wild tangles of blackberry vines. A white 'For Sale' sign was barely visible in the snarls.

"'Sup."

Oliver turned to a figure seated on the rooftop behind him. Despite the chilly rain, he wore only a steel gray t-shirt, dark jeans, and muddy Converse. His arms were crossed atop his knees. Oliver made sure not to react to the sour odor flooding his nostrils.

"Hey," Oliver said to Dean.

"How was the interrogation?" Dean asked.

Oliver huffed. "The usual. You coming?"

"Do I ever?" asked Dean. "Somebody needs to keep watch, anyway."

Oliver nodded. "See you in a minute."

He stepped over the side of the house, flipping under the eave so that he hung inverted like a bat. More memories… of watching from here as a door opened, as hands opened the first gift he'd given her, a new camera….

Oliver dropped to the ground. The basement door was locked, dead-bolted from the inside. To the right, a window was covered with plywood. It appeared to be

<20>

thoroughly nailed shut, but only the four corner nails were actually sunk into the wall. The rest were just show. Oliver peeled the plywood carefully away so as not to bend the nails, leaned it against the base of the wall, and wormed through the narrow space. There were still a few glass shards sticking up here and there, but Oliver had learned how to avoid them. *Without oven mitts*, he thought to himself, considering not for the first time that now he was the intruder sneaking into the abandoned house, as she had once been.

The cobwebs seemed to double every time he visited. He brushed the gray curtains aside, moving through the pitch black basement, between walls of cardboard boxes, until he reached the open space, bordered on two sides by boxes, on the third by a rusty washer and dryer, and on the fourth by a double sink. Water dripped from the leaky faucet. Oliver inspected the room but saw disappointedly that things were just as he'd left them. The pile of darkroom supplies on the shelf beside the sink, the strings that crisscrossed the ceiling strung with black and white photos…

Emalie's space. Her presence was everywhere.

After she and her parents and Great Aunt Kathleen had left for the old west town of Arcana and the year 1868, a realtor friend of Aunt Kathleen's had come by and put that 'For Sale' sign out front. It was just for show, though. The house was being held until they came back.

When Oliver first returned here, he'd found Emalie's piles of photographs beneath the sink. There were hundreds

<21>

in all, and Oliver had strung some across the ceiling, taped more to the box sides around him and all over the washer and dryer. He'd tiled the floor with others.

He sat down now in the middle of the darkroom space, a collage all around him; it was like being in Emalie's mind, the world she'd seen through her camera eye. Over by the sink were some of the photos from the abandoned house above Oliver's home. From that first December morning, the chance encounter that had changed everything, set them off on so many adventures... and led to her leaving.

There was one thing in the room that wasn't Emalie's. In the middle of the floor was a foot-tall box, made of delicate wood and hinged at its sides so that it could be folded up and stored flat when not in use. Oliver flipped open the lid and reached inside without looking. His fingers brushed through the contents, making a quiet clattering sound, and emerged with a small, silver teardrop-shaped earring.

He held the earring, sniffed it gently, winced at the memories it unearthed, and then placed it on the floor, inside a small circle drawn with rose-colored gypsum sand. Then, he stood, cocked his ear toward the far corner of the room, and crept away. He returned to his seat a moment later, his hands cupped in front of him.

He opened them, revealing a tiny gray mouse lying on its side, unmoving except for the rapid rise and fall of its chest. It was alive, yet Oliver had stilled its soul, which put the creature in such a state of fear that it became frozen in a kind of paralyzed state.

<22>

The stilling gaze was a new skill which Oliver and his classmates had been learning this year. First, you identified the scents and force signatures of fear in the creature, and then you tried to project the essence of these feelings back through your gaze, which literally froze the creature in fright. You couldn't perform it on anything large, like a human, until you had your demon—Oliver had tried it on Dean one time, but Dean just laughed and made fun of Oliver's "serious" gaze—so his teacher, Mr. VanWick, had them practice on smaller creatures like mice or lizards.

Oliver held the little mouse over the earring and with his other hand, extended his index finger. *"Ensacrifetthhh..."* he hissed quietly, employing the ancient Skrit word for 'in sacrifice,' as in, in service to a greater cause. Then, he drew his long, sharp fingernail across the little mouse's neck.

When three drops of blood had fallen into the circle, he produced a tissue, wrapped up the mouse, then paused. The scent was strong.... He couldn't resist a snack before slipping the mouse's body away in his pocket. *She would have thought that was gross*, Oliver thought, and it only heightened his empty feeling.

"It's ready," he said quietly in the dark.

The basement was silent for a moment, then there was a slight rush of wind. Two forms shimmered into existence before Oliver, one of dark wispy smoke, the other of shimmering white light, with silver edges that threw off blue sparks.

Hey guys, Oliver thought to Jenette and Nathan.

Hey, Nathan replied. Oliver felt that familiar warmth

<23>

from his presence; Nathan was Oliver's soul. Oliver was the only vampire in history whose soul was still attached to him. All other vampire children had been created in a lab, and never had souls to begin with, and all adult vampires had demons, which they received when they were sired, meaning turned from humans into vampires. The demon's arrival severed the connection with the soul, and the soul journeyed out of the world.

Unlike all the other vampire children, Oliver had actually been specially sired, as had Bane, when they were infants. So, Oliver did have a soul, and because he hadn't received a demon yet—vampire children didn't get their demons until their teen years, when their bodies were strong enough—his soul had lingered on, separated from him but not completely.

They could only risk seeing each other briefly these days. If Half-Light found Nathan, they would surely destroy him. Jenette and the other wraiths kept him safe out at the Shoals, a borderland on the edge of the world.

It was nice to see Nathan. Oliver liked to feel that warmth that was also his own, and yet Nathan's proximity also reminded him of the hollow spaces inside him. In the one moment when they'd been able to join together, in the house of Oliver's birth parents, Oliver had felt so complete, as if Nathan filled those empty places, and he couldn't help wishing for that feeling again. The idea of *wanting* to have a soul, maybe even to be alive, was something that other vampires would surely turn up their noses at. After all, humans were so short-lived, so frail, so ruled by the

<24>

love/hate power of Finity. Who would want to be a lowly living thing?

Still, Oliver did. But it was impossible. And so having Nathan around, though it was nice, also reminded Oliver of what could never be.

Hi Oliver, said Jenette. She circled the room in a flurry. Wraiths were spirits tied to the world by their grief. Instead of flowing out of the world upon their death, they lingered because of sorrow and guilt, until they became trapped. Jenette had originally been hired to slay Oliver, but since then they'd become friends. The wraiths didn't want Oliver to fulfill his destiny of opening the Nexia gate, as it would destroy the loved ones they grieved for. They had helped Oliver and his friends on a number of occasions.

Any word? Jenette asked.

Nothing, said Oliver. That was his answer to most things these days.

Jenette floated over. Her wispy hand rubbed Oliver's shoulder. *I'm sorry.* Oliver could definitely hear the little note of hope in Jenette's voice. She tried to be supportive, but her crush on Oliver was no secret, not that she or Oliver ever mentioned it. They had even kissed once, well, Jenette had kissed Oliver on the cheek, back in the Space Needle. They didn't mention that, either.

How are you doing? Oliver asked.

Jenette sighed. It sounded like wind whistling through a crack in a wall. *Okay, I guess.*

<25>

Oliver was more careful with his next question. *How is she?*

Not good, said Jenette. She sniffled. *I saw her last week, and she was getting an MRI. The doctor said something about it spreading....* Jenette's mother had been diagnosed with cancer. It was bad. She had been smoking for decades, so the cancer wasn't a huge shock but it was still terrible for Jenette, especially since there was nothing she could do. Jenette had died in a house fire over thirty years ago, when she was only eleven. She still looked about that age. Wraiths were able to make themselves apparent to the living, but in the past when Jenette had tried to visit her mother, it had only terrified her.

I'm sorry, said Oliver.

I know, said Jenette. *Thanks.*

Time is short, Nathan reminded them.

Okay, said Oliver. *Let's get this over with.*

Nathan sat beside him. His warmth seeped into Oliver's shoulder. Together, they reached down and cupped their hands over the earring, Oliver's on top of Nathan's. Jenette put one hand atop theirs, and then twisted her body and extended her other hand behind her. It seemed to encounter a ripple, as if the air were liquid.

The ripple parted to reveal a hole in reality. Through it poured the haze-gray light of the Shoals, a beach on the edge of the world. Oliver could hear the waves lapping against the sand and rocks.

There was a hissing cry, and a black, bony hand draped

<26>

in ragged cloth shot through the hole. It grabbed Jenette by her wrist, which was still fleshy and nearly-human looking compared to this ancient wraith.

Jenette gasped at the strength of the hold, but then nodded. *Ready.*

Oliver closed his eyes and began the Skrit incantation for the *Sonarias* enchantment. "*Contatennn....*" The spell was somewhat like a homing pigeon, or a search command. They were sending a message out along the force beams, designed to attract itself to Emalie's presence, which was why each time they performed the spell, they had to use one of Oliver's precious mementoes, the trinkets and notes he'd collected during their time together.

This enchantment was actually part-Orani in origin; Oliver had found it in Emalie's notebooks. She would have been much better at it, but using the power of the wraiths, they did okay. The wraiths acted as a kind of amplifier to get the message out across time and space.

"*Trasmuthhh....*" Oliver felt warmth prickling up through his arms. Orange sparks began to fly out from their hands. The connection had been made, and now it was time to send the message itself. Oliver aimed his mind, and thought the words, slowly and carefully... *Hope you are well... Be in touch....*

It had been agonizing trying to decide exactly what to say. Oliver's first instinct had been to say 'come back,' but that seemed too... desperate or something. And he'd obviously thought to say 'miss you,' but that was, well, just something he didn't want to admit out loud. Because,

<27>

was she missing him? Probably, but... how could he know for sure? And there were other words too, that he wanted to admit even less, about his feelings....

There was a whooshing of energy, light coursing from their hands, through Jenette, and then a blinding cry from a hundred wraiths, like icicles of sound. Then silence. Dark.

Done, said Jenette. The wraith released her wrist. The hole into the Shoals closed. Oliver sighed. He always hoped for some kind of instantaneous reply, some kind of sign that somewhere out there in the universe, Emalie could hear him, but instead there was only the silence of the basement, the sound of rain outside.

Nathan patted his shoulder. *It's all we can do*, he said. *I know.*

Something knocked distantly on the roof. Three raps of a fist: Dean's warning that he'd spotted an occupied creature approaching.

Go, said Oliver to Nathan and Jenette, and as Nathan nodded and stepped away, Oliver frowned at the loss of that warmth.

We'll let you know, said Jenette, *if we hear anything.*
Okay.

Nathan and Jenette joined hands and winked out of sight, back to the safety of the gray beach.

Oliver's head fell. His shoulders slumped. Outside, fresh sheets of rain began to pebble the basement window. *Miss you*, he thought, and wondered if he should have just said that in the message. He pulled the box toward

<28>

him, dropping his hand inside. He felt a fuzzy moment of weightlessness as his hand scraped through the objects. Hair bands, notes she'd left under their desk at school....

He slammed the box, knocking it across the room, its contents scattering. This sucked! Why did he even come here? It was pointless. Emalie was gone, and it wasn't like she'd taken a trip to Hawaii or something. She'd left this timespace altogether! There was no way he was going to get in touch with her. And she was never coming back.

She will, he thought, trying to convince himself. *You have to have hope.* Like he'd had when she left, on that September evening...

But as Oliver stood and began picking up his Emalie collection, he considered that that evening was a long time ago, now, and his feeling of hope had long since dimmed.

There were only a few items left to put back in the box. They would have only a few more tries at the Sonarias enchantment. Once a month they'd performed it, when the moon was new, from September to November. But though Emalie had left in late September, they hadn't been trying for just for two months....

It had been over two years.

<29>

Chapter 3

COHESION

'Anything new on the Triad?" Dean asked as they leaped from one rooftop to the next, making their way to school.

"No," Oliver muttered, and he felt another fierce surge of frustration grip him. There was a satellite dish on the roof they'd just landed on and Oliver kicked it, shattering it into multiple parts.

Ugh! It was always the same! During their first year together, there had been so much promise: discovering truths, solving mysteries, getting closer and closer to changing Oliver's destiny. Everything had been scary and overwhelming and yet, looking back, it had all been an incredible adventure, as exciting as it was ominous, and then... nothing. Two years of nothing! It was as if all that momentum had just faded away. Sometimes it seemed hard to believe that it had all really even happened.

They leapt again, this time pausing on a flat apartment

<30>

roof. The rain was pelting now. Below, a bus roared by. They vaulted down onto it and sat on the roof.

"I'm beginning to wonder," said Oliver, "if the Triad even exists, or what."

On the night that Emalie left, they had received the oracle Selene's final message, hidden within a firefly. Oliver still remembered it: *There exist three elements known as the Triad of Finity. They are most cleverly hidden....*

"You will know how to find them when the first speaks to you," said Dean, remembering the end of Selene's message. "I still don't get what that means."

Oliver just shrugged. "If something was going to speak to us, you'd think it would have happened by now." He huffed to himself.

"What?"

Oliver shook his head. "Why hasn't she gotten in touch?" He meant Emalie.

"I don't know," said Dean. "Maybe she's trying, but it's hard. Or someone's stopping her."

"Or..." Oliver didn't want to finish the thought.

"Yeah," said Dean, thinking it too.

They'd already discussed it a number of times: How there had been that photo in Selene's bedroom at the Asylum Colony that showed Selene and Emalie's mom standing together. How on the back it said: *Selene and Phoebe, Guardians of the Muse, March 14, 1868.* How back when Oliver was first researching the sunlight slayings, the vampire codex had told him that the entire town of Arcana had been destroyed in 1868 due to a mass

<31>

hysteria that was supposedly caused by the Orani.

And so, what if Emalie had gone to Arcana and died, or been killed or whatever, before she'd even had a chance to get in touch with them? There was no evidence that this had happened, but also no proof that it hadn't.

It drove Oliver crazy, lots of thoughts tumbling through his brain at once: Her kissing him, how he should have kissed her back, should have grabbed her and held on, told her how he felt, even that he lov— But he'd just stood there and let her go. *Like a little lamb*, Bane would have said.

"I wish we could go after her," said Dean, as he had many times before.

"Tsss," Oliver hissed in sullen agreement. Over the last two years, they'd had plenty of time to research the possibilities for getting to Arcana themselves. Traveling through space-time was no easy thing. Traditionally, only certain higher demons could do it, and they always had to secure permission from a Time Merchynt who existed across four-dimensional space. Emalie and her family had used just such a being, Chronius, who granted access to time portals in the form of his fingernail.

Last January, already tired of waiting around, Oliver and Dean had climbed down into the Yomi and asked Chronius if he could send them back to Arcana, but he merely dismissed them with a wave of his smoky, time-blurred hand.

"Look at you," he had whispered. "A vampire and a zombie. You have no form of payment that I could

<32>

possibly want." Emalie and the Orani had apparently been able to give Chronius information from the minds of his competitors in the Yomi.

"We're never going to find her," Oliver muttered.

They sat silently in the rain.

"Nnnn," Dean moaned quietly a moment later. Oliver turned to see him wincing and scratching brusquely at his forearm, his long yellow fingernails leaving black streaks across his blotched purple-and-yellow skin.

"Bad?" Oliver asked.

"Yeah," said Dean. He scratched harder, and now a patch of skin tore free. Black fluid dripped down his wet arm. Oliver's nose twitched at a tangy smell of decay, like spoiled milk mixed with rancid meat; he was getting better at not showing his disgust at this, but it wasn't easy.

"Antibiotics aren't helping?"

Dean just shook his head. "The only thing that helps is the rain. The cold, too. And, well, you know...."

Oliver nodded grimly. Over the last two years, Dean's zombie condition had been getting worse: the necrosis of his skin, the festering bacteria that no amount of antibiotics or toxins could totally cure. Rain eased the near constant itching he felt, but the moisture led to mold problems too severe to be treated even with the pure quartz sand baths his mom Tammy prepared for him.

The fact was that even though zombies were more long-lived than vampires, eventually they tended to rot down to the bare bones (they usually kept their eyeballs and brains, though, along with various kinds of bone fungi, which

<33>

made for an appearance that even a vampire could find unsettling). It was the natural way of their existence. But it was happening to Dean faster than most, because there was only one thing that somewhat staved off the effects of time, and it was the one thing that Dean swore not to eat.

Human brains. But much like human blood for a vampire, once a zombie had a taste for brains, there was no turning back. The desire became an unquenchable thirst that overtook any other kind of rational thought. The only way to keep from becoming a moaning brute like the other zombies was to resist. Which meant living in near constant rot and pain. Both options sucked.

"I'm not going to be one of them," said Dean quietly. This was something he repeated often.

"I know," said Oliver, but he had to wonder: how long could Dean hold out? He was only a zombie after all. His destiny was inevitable, just like Oliver's destiny to get a demon.

On nights like this one, Oliver couldn't help entertaining a certain thought: Maybe opening the Gate and ending all this was actually the best way things could turn out, at least for the two of them. Dean's suffering would be over. And Oliver would be a fully demonized vampire, so his guilt and worry would be gone. There'd be no more yearning for his soul, no more emptiness or confusion, and there'd be no more missing Emalie....

They reached school. Rodrigo let them in the back door. Oliver waited as Dean ducked downstairs to a bathroom, where he changed into a dry school uniform that he kept

<34>

stashed in the ceiling panels: white shirt, black pants and a tie, just like Oliver's.

They headed upstairs, passing the glowing demonic forms of the grotesqua dancing around the walls. They reached the second floor and pushed through crowds of younger vampires who jumped away, mainly due to Dean's smell, but also because Oliver and Dean were in the 8th Pentath now: the oldest kids.

They passed the classroom where Oliver had attended 7th Pentath, and headed up a smaller set of stairs. At the top, a narrow door to the school's attic stood open. This was their classroom.

Dean used to go to a home school with two other students: a zombie girl named Autumn Fitch and a human boy named Sledge. Autumn's mother, a zombie shaman named Ariana, taught the classes in Dean's basement.

It had been a good arrangement, until last spring, when Dean's family took a trip out to Spokane for the April school vacation to visit family (Dean had traveled in the trunk to spare his siblings from his odor). Dean's mother, Tammy, agreed to let Ariana hold class for Autumn and Sledge while they were gone. But one night, Autumn and Sledge, as they often did, got into a nasty fight about American football, specifically over the finer points of the Seahawks' offseason moves. Zombies in general, and Sledge too, were huge football fans. If Sledge could have kept himself in a normal school, he would definitely have been on a team.

The fight spiraled; they started pushing one another,

<35>

and Autumn ended up biting Sledge. A zombie bite was infectious, and would turn a human in about forty eight hours. But the smell of fresh blood led Autumn and Ariana to agree that letting Sledge become a zombie would be cruel, so instead they made a meal of Sledge's brains and entrails, and then, in a state of bloodlust, they left without cleaning up and proceeded to go on a rampage around the neighborhood. A disgusted vampire couple passing by beheaded Ariana, and Autumn barely escaped, minus her right arm.

So that was the end of the home school. The Aunders' returned home to a grim reminder of what Dean really was, of what he was bound to become. Dean hadn't seen Autumn, and things hadn't been the same at home, since.

Of course, having a zombie in a vampire school should have been unthinkable, except in Dean's case there were two exceptions: First, Half-Light liked having Dean and Oliver in the same place, to keep an eye on them, and second, there was a new student in the 8th Pentath who liked having him around, too.

"Minion!"

Dean was just inside the door when his shoulders slumped. "Ugh, what already?" He moaned, rolling his eyes. He looked up at the ceiling miserably.

"I need my sweatshirt!" called Lythia LeRoux. She snapped her fingers expectantly.

"Get your own stupid sweatshirt!" Dean muttered, yet he obediently shuffled over to Lythia's desk, picked up her sweatshirt, and threw it up to her. "There, happy?"

<36>

Lythia scowled, brushing her upside down hair out of her eyes. "Don't talk back to me, slave!" she shouted.

"Will if I want to," mumbled Dean, walking away.

"Give it a rest, Lythia," Oliver snapped at her.

"Shut up, Nocturne!" Lythia hissed. She glared at him menacingly, her eyes glowing, but they were only a pale blue now, not the lavender they'd once been, and her look didn't have the same effect it once had.

"Whatever," said Oliver, waving a hand at her dismissively as he continued across the room.

Lythia snarled, but didn't say anything further. Instead, she turned back to her ceiling-mates and leaned in, whispering conspiratorially.

It had been a long two years, from the middle of the last year of 7th Pentath into this second year of 8th, with Lythia LeRoux as one of his classmates. She'd lost her demon during the Anointment ceremony, and so had been rendered just another middle school student. Of course, she hadn't lost her attitude, or her evil streak, but she had lost all of her advanced vampire powers, along with that dizzying demon presence she used to have. She was still technically Dean's master, and could still command him to do her bidding, but without her demon strength, Dean could somewhat resist her, or at least complain loudly, and carry out his instructions lackadaisically and with almost no enthusiasm.

"So annoying," Dean muttered now as he walked over to the far wall.

The attic was a long, triangular room with only two

<37>

circular windows, one in the center of each end wall. The corners were piled with a hundred years of junk from the human school: old computers and typewriters, outdated globes and maps, microscopes and broken chairs. Hidden in these piles were the necessary vampire class supplies: weapons, texts, and importantly, the set of triple reinforced titanium shackles.

Class mainly took place on a circle of thick floor pillows, centered around a design of concentric circles made from different colored crystal sands. When the Pentath had begun, there had been seventeen pillows including one for Mr. VanWick, eighteen counting Dean's, which was over by the wall. Now, only eight remained. Ten students had received their *vampyr* demons and moved on to high school.

Oliver sat down cross-legged on his pillow and unloaded his supplies from his backpack: a black candle, matches, a pair of heavily tinted welder's goggles, a small ivory-handled knife with a short but lethal two-inch blade, and a slim black leather volume with a single Skrit symbol on the front, meaning Demonology and History.

Oliver glanced back at Dean. They made a habit of not talking during school, as it could be assumed that anything they said was being monitored not only by Half-Light, but also by the little gang of students assembled on the ceiling.

Their whispers attracted Oliver's attention now. Beside Lythia sat Theo and Maggots. Theo and Lythia had been fast friends, especially after Theo's girlfriend Kym had gotten her demon last spring and promptly dumped him.

<38>

She was dating a high school boy now who'd nicknamed himself The Talon. Everybody else from Theo's old circle was gone, too, except for Maggots.

Oliver couldn't tell what they were talking about, but he stretched his senses and tried to hear:

"… forces…" he heard Theo mumbling.

"… closer to… radiance…"

"What about the Legion meeting?" Maggots blurted out.

"Shut up!" Lythia hissed as Theo socked Maggots in the shoulder. Lythia flashed a quick glance at Oliver, catching him watching. "Mind your own business, Nocturne!" she snapped. "Go back to daydreaming about your long lost bloodbag!"

Oliver narrowed his eyes at her, but didn't reply. Instead, he filed away these latest tidbits of information. Oliver couldn't be sure what, but Lythia and Theo were definitely up to something. There were lots of secretive moments like this lately. He'd heard them mention the word 'legion' before, but not 'radiance.'

Berthold Welch crept through the door, slouching his undersized self across the room, hoping to avoid any interaction with the ceiling crowd. Back in 7th Pentath, he'd always been the target for tripping and other violent pranks. They were all too old for those kinds of kids' games now, but the verbal taunting could be twice as biting. Yet the ceiling crowd paid no attention to him tonight.

"Hey Oliver," said Berthold, sitting on the pillow beside him.

<39>

"Hey," said Oliver.

"Think tonight will be the night?" Berthold asked.

Oliver rolled his eyes. "Probably not." Berthold had been asking that question practically every night for the last two years. "But I guess you never know."

"I hope it's my night," Berthold said hopefully as he got out his supplies.

Oliver felt like telling Berthold, *don't bet on it*, but he didn't. You could sort of tell when kids were ready to get their demon. They'd dress older, be more obnoxious, and their demon dreams would be in full swing. Berthold was nowhere near any of those things. Oliver wasn't, either. He still hadn't had a demon dream since that night, almost three years ago now, when Dean had been killed. Then again, kids like Theo and Lythia had attitudes like they should have been demon-ready years ago, and yet they were still here, so maybe you never knew.

When the last student arrived, Oliver leaned to Berthold. "I think we know whose night it's going to be."

Carly had appeared in the doorway. Her entrance set off an intense round of whispers from the ceiling trio. In the past, these whispers might have been because of Carly's lack of fashion sense—compared to other vampire girls, she was never very put-together—or her shy mannerisms, but this time they were different. Something had changed over the last few days. The mouse-quiet girl that Oliver had always gotten along with had suddenly transformed.

"Hey guys," Carly said with a lazy drawl as she slouched in the doorway. She made a little salute, her mouth

<40>

smacking on gum. "How's it hangin'?" She sauntered across the room, her leather bag and a skinny black jacket falling off her shoulder, revealing a teal tank top. Spiked-heel magenta boots clicked on the uneven wood floor.

Oliver didn't get it. This was the same girl who, up until about three weeks ago, had always arrived in sweatpants and oversized flannel shirts, her hair a rat's nest. Now her hair was slicked down straight and dyed cobalt blue.

She dropped down onto her pillow, legs thrown out straight, crossing her boots. "Hey Oliver," she said around her gum. "How's your mopey self doing?"

"Fine," said Oliver quietly. He was sad to be losing Carly, but these were the clear signs of a student on the cusp of cohesion: the bonding with a *vampyr* demon.

The only thing weird about it was how fast it had come on. Seriously, just last Friday, she'd been the same old Carly. But then she'd showed up Monday completely different, and changing at a furious pace.

Oliver glanced up and saw Lythia and Theo eyeing her, clearly jealous.

Cohesion was supposed to take at least a couple months, sometimes a full year, but Carly was the fourth case in their class of this accelerated cohesion happening in mere weeks, if not days. All in the last couple months. It was weird.

"Good evening students." Mr. VanWick swept into the room, closing the door behind him and pulling off his long black coat. "Let's begin." He wrapped a black ceremonial robe over his tweed suit and sat cross-legged on a pillow.

<41>

Pulling the hood over his head, he struck a match and lit a black candle in front of him.

"First, the meditation." All the students took their seats and lit their candles. He reached forward, his smooth white fingers curled around a jagged black crystal. He scraped this against the outermost sand circle, made of pink crystal powder. It ignited in a brilliant ring of low pink flames.

"Remember, the demon seeks a vessel," he said in a low voice. "You are that vessel. We search among the ethers to find our demon, the one that is meant for us. *Vampyrethhh...*" he breathed.

"*Vampyrethhh...*" the students repeated. Everyone closed their eyes, even Oliver. He didn't want to, but not participating meant staying after school, and possibly extra visits from Mr. Crevlyn.

"We begin the search for our demon in the familiar world," said Mr. VanWick. "Step back inside your mind, search the dark corners. You are looking for a door...."

They all spoke at once, their answers part of the cadence of the ritual. "I see a door," they said.

Oliver saw a door in his mind, too. He was treading down a hall with burgundy carpet, its walls solid yet also made of stars. Ahead was the door. Oliver had seen it before: solid black wood with a silver knob and a white Skrit symbol etched into it. This was the symbol of the demon who had once been meant for Bane, but was now meant for Oliver, one of the most ancient and powerful demons in all of history: Illisius.

<42>

"Open the door," instructed Mr. VanWick, "and enter the room."

Each of the vampire children were experiencing something similar to Oliver: opening a door inside their minds and walking into a room with dark-wood bookshelves, a desk and comfortable chair, and a wide, diamond-shaped window. This was the visual image of the demon's place in each vampire's mind, their entry point.

Oliver entered the room. His body shook with nerves. To come here was to tempt his destiny. One day he would enter this room and it would begin: through the window he would see his demon's history, as Illisius, in effect, downloaded himself into Oliver's mind.

But tonight, just like every other time he'd ever been here, what he saw beyond the empty bookshelves, beyond the black desk, out the wide window, was a land made of blood red rock, crooked spires of amethyst and jade here and there, and nearby, a giant statue head with gold coin eyes, lying on the ground. Everything was bathed in golden light from something just out of Oliver's view, something glowing brilliantly: the Gate. This was Nexia, where he was destined to go to fulfill his destiny. Same as always. The view gave him a chill, but it was also a small comfort. Cohesion had not begun.

"Does anyone see anything new?" asked Mr. VanWick. Oliver heard him distantly, out on the surface of his consciousness, like a voice through a thick window.

There was a frustrated sigh. "Still the sacking of Babylon," said Lythia disappointedly. Her cohesion had

<43>

begun, but it was early, and going slowly, as it was supposed to. Her demon had apparently been instrumental in the military efforts of Cyrus the Great and the Persians during the ancient Battle of Opis. She'd been stuck in this same place for awhile. The dreams tended to move forward through history chronologically, reaching the present as cohesion got closer.

"Still the Spanish Inquisition for me," muttered Theo. His demon had been fond of wagering on these types of bloody events. He'd been there for a few weeks, too.

"Just fog," said Berthold sadly. His cohesion hadn't started.

"I see something new…" Carly said with a shaking voice, "a field of blood."

Whispers shot around the room.

"Go on," said Mr. VanWick.

"The bodies are fresh, scattered like trash," Carly whispered. "Skulls, ribcages…. Everything is crushed."

"You are seeing through Dylea's eyes," said Mr. VanWick reassuringly.

The whispers solidified into murmurs. Oliver heard Theo cursing under his breath with jealousy.

"What is the weaponry?"

"There are trenches," said Carly. "Rifles and bayonets, cannons, artillery streaks in the sky. Some of the bodies have gas masks on."

"Return," instructed Mr. VanWick.

Oliver left his room. It took some effort; even though he didn't want his demon, there was something soothing

<44>

about the place, a feeling of completeness that was actually somewhat similar to what he felt when Nathan was around, as if having a demon would make him feel more whole, too. He pushed back to the surface of his mind. He opened his eyes and saw the rest of his class doing the same.

Mr. VanWick had picked up his copy of the slim black textbook. Oliver opened his. The book was blank inside, as was everyone else's.

"*Revelethh Dylea*," Mr. VanWick whispered to the book. The same image began to appear in everyone's book. Text and pictures bled onto the pages. There was a detailed sketch of Dylea, a tall, shrouded demon with blue skin, and text titled "France, 1917."

"Dylea was soul-collecting at the Battle of the Marne," said Mr. VanWick, reading the text. He looked at Carly, and Oliver noticed the slight furrow of his brow. "Dylea's timeline is nearing yours." He shook his head. "It's astonishing; just yesterday you saw her in the French Revolution. That's over one hundred years in just a night... but, I guess it's nothing new for this class."

"For *some* of us," Lythia muttered with a scowl. Oliver glanced at her and found her staring directly at him. She looked like she was studying him, and as soon as she saw that Oliver had noticed her, she looked away.

"All right, back to your rooms," instructed Mr. VanWick. "We will continue the observation, and deepen the connection." He reached out and used the black crystal to ignite the next inner sand circle, this one made

<45>

of lavender powder. "Concentrate," he commanded.

Oliver sank back into his mind, back into the hallway, to the door, and back into the room, walking inside like he always did—

But it had changed.

Over on the left bookshelf, a handful of black books were stacked neatly, held in place by an iron bookend in the shape of a brooding gargoyle, and out the window...

Nexia was gone.

For the first time in over a year of cohesion sessions, the view out the diamond-shaped window was different.

Oh no, Oliver thought, his gut writhing with nerves. *It's starting.*

<46>

Chapter 4

THE VAMPYR

Oliver saw an endless, luminous gray fog stretching from one edge of the window to the other. It was thick and undulating up and down. There was something solid in the corner of the window: the edge of a metal railing. Below that was lapping water, but not normal water. This substance was black and clear, with stars beneath its surface. It reminded Oliver of the water at the Shoals. Edge water. The material between worlds.

Oliver understood, as Mr. VanWick had explained, that the books on the shelves were the visual representation of Illisius' memories being added to Oliver's mind. And what he was seeing out the window was the view out of Illisius' eyes, from some time in the past. It looked like he was in the process of crossing from one world to another, as higher demons could do. But where was this, and when?

Since this was the first dream, this should be a memory from long ago, except, this wasn't technically Oliver's first

<47>

dream. He'd already been visited by Illisius on the night that Dean had died in the school gym. And that dream had been different than a normal cohesion dream because Illisius had actually spoken to him, shown him Nexia, the Gate.... So, Oliver had no idea if his dreams would follow the normal pattern of the other students. But either way, the fact that he was having another dream could not be a good thing.

The ship bobbed in the starry water, fog blowing by—

"AAAAAAA!"

The scream tore through Oliver's mind. The window and room blurred away. Oliver was sucked back up to reality. He opened his eyes to find that everyone else had returned to the classroom, too. There was a blinding light to his right.

"Get the shackles!" Mr. VanWick instructed tersely, leaping to his feet. Across the circle, Maggots dutifully spun and rushed to the piles of junk behind him. "Everyone! Goggles on!"

Oliver slipped his large black welder's goggles over his eyes. The room disappeared in a dark green tint, except for the brilliant light. It was thrashing about, just on the other side of Berthold, who was edging away. The light was golden with rainbow swirls arcing around it like Oliver had seen in Dr. Vincent's force resonance imager. In the center of that light was Carly, pulled to a standing position, floating, her feet a few inches off the floor.

"Keep your distance," Mr. VanWick advised, his own goggles over his eyes. As everyone backed away, he took

<48>

the chains from Maggots, a set of four thick, titanium shackles connected by heavy, jangling loops, and moved toward Carly. He quickly fastened the shackles to her ankles, then wrists. Just as he was connecting the last one, a demonic, multi-pitched screech tore through the room. Mr. VanWick leapt backward, latching the shackles with a bulky padlock to a huge ring that was bolted in the floor.

And then the *vampyr* arrived. A fluid silver form burst into existence in a blinding flash. It slithered through the air like a shark, all gleaming movement and blazing red eyes, its fangs bared, its shrieking endless.

Even having seen this before, first when Bane's *vampyr* emerged from Emalie during the Anointment, and then in all the times since when students had received theirs in class, Oliver still found himself shrinking away from the sight. He knew from Mr. VanWick's teachings that there was no danger of the *vampyr* ending up inside anyone other than Carly; each *vampyr* was specifically matched with its vampire vessel.

Technically, 'sentenced' was a better word, because a *vampyr* was a demon that had been convicted of wrongdoing by the Architects. The word *vampyr* literally translated to 'criminal' in many worlds. These demons weren't convicted because they were evil, at least by any human standard, but there were many rules that governed the higher dimensions, most of which had to do with maintaining world boundary integrity and the balance of influence.

The *vampyr* hated being sentenced to eventually die

<49>

stuck inside a human shell. A vampire's life of four-to-five hundred years was incredibly short when compared to the near-infinite existences of demons. And a vampire's set of powers, while amazing to a human, was insultingly limited compared to, for example, Dylea's, the demon who had been sentenced to Carly.

And so there was danger in this moment of cohesion, these few seconds while Dylea was in the room but not yet inside Carly. She was furious, frenzied. If you got too close, she might rip your head off just to cope with her own agony.

Once the *vampyr* was in its host, it mellowed. Dylea and Carly would blend, influencing one another, and like any demon, Dylea would quickly figure out how to make the best of the situation. But in this moment, watching a loose *vampyr* thrash and spin in fury like a trapped animal, Oliver could see why generations of vampires had been searching for a way to break free of this existence. This creature would give anything to open the Gate and change its fate.

"Almost there," said Mr. VanWick.

The *vampyr* spiraled closer and closer to Carly. Her eyes were closed, her body seemingly in a trance. Still, her mouth was twisted in a grimace, like this wasn't fun for her either.

The shrieking increased, causing a humming headache that speared through Oliver's brain, and then finally the creature wrapped in on Carly and sucked into her body through the top of her chest, just below her neck, the same

<50>

area where Oliver had once seen Emalie's soul depart.

Silence. The red eyes, the silver form, the gold light and rainbow swirls all vanished, and the room was plunged into darkness. Everyone's candles had been extinguished in the rush.

Oliver pulled off his goggles. Carly was lying on the floor, curled in a ball. Her eyes flickered open. They had been brown. Now they glowed bright ruby. She blinked hard and stood up, then surveyed the room dazedly, looking from one of them to the next. Her gaze fell on Oliver, and its contempt felt familiar. He could practically hear her thinking that they were all pathetic lambs.

"*Tch*," Carly clucked to herself, hands on her hips. "Later, kiddies," she muttered with a half smile. "I need some fresh meat."

She turned and sauntered out of middle school forever.

"Lucky," said Berthold quietly, crawling back to his pillow seat beside Oliver.

"Let's take a short break," said Mr. Van Wick. "We'll begin again in a few minutes." He had produced a leather notebook, the official Cohesion Log, and had it open in his lap, but Oliver saw him staring at the door, his brow again in a curious furrow, like something wasn't quite right. Oliver guessed that it had something to do with the speed of it. Carly's cohesion, beginning to end, had taken barely a week.

Oliver heard whispering voices and glanced across the dwindling circle—only five of them left now—to where Lythia was talking in Theo's ear. They were both glaring

<51>

at Oliver, and Theo was nodding grimly.

"What?" said Oliver, hating that feeling that someone was talking about him.

Lythia leveled a lethal gaze at him. "You know what, Nocturne."

"No, I don't," Oliver snapped back.

"Oh, whatever." Lythia rolled her eyes dramatically.

"Guess you'll be next," Theo muttered at him. He looked around the circle. "And then that will be that for the rest of us."

"What are you talking about?" Oliver asked.

"Just mind your own business!" Lythia snarled. "And leave us alone."

"Fine." Oliver stood and headed for the door. He glanced over at Dean. "Wanna take a walk?"

Dean got up, stumbling against the wall. Mr. VanWick hadn't provided him with goggles, so the cohesions always left him somewhat blind for awhile. He walked over to Oliver, rubbing at his eyes.

"Minion! Sock the pretty perfect one for me!" Lythia shouted.

"Oh shut up and do it yourself!" Dean moaned, but then he dutifully turned and swung a fist at Oliver. Luckily, due to his partial blindness, he only grazed Oliver's shoulder. "Sorry," he added.

As they reached the door, Oliver turned back to Lythia. "Happy?"

But there was no trace of satisfaction on Lythia's face. In fact, right at that moment, she was looking at Oliver

<52>

like she simply hated him. All that old superiority she'd had with a demon was gone. In fact, she almost looked… helpless. "No," she grunted, and turned back to Theo with a flip of her hair.

Oliver and Dean wandered downstairs and back up, not speaking. Oliver's thoughts floated from one thing to the next: the images of Illisius' travels in his mind, the sight of Carly getting her demon, the lonely feeling of Emalie's basement, even that strange, bitter anger from Lythia, and also the sense that she was up to something again. Some secret she was planning with Theo.

What did he mean by saying Oliver was probably next? For cohesion? Oliver hated the return of that old feeling, like he was missing something that had to do with him. But that feeling paled in comparison to his worry about the dream. For years, really for his entire existence, he'd known this day would come: growing up, getting a demon, and while most days he liked to believe that he had more time, that he could stay the way he was and that the future was far away, tonight he knew better.

The future was here, ready or not. And without any clues about Emalie or undoing his destiny, this truly felt like the beginning of the end.

<53>

Chapter 5

SECRET PLANS

Close to dawn, Oliver reclined in his open coffin, reading. He could hear Phlox upstairs readying dinner.

The book Oliver was flipping through was from the human library; Dean had found it, after their searches in the vampire library for anything more about Arcana had come up empty. Actually, the exact message the vampire catalogue had delivered was: *That topic is restricted.*

Dean had found something though, one random reference to Arcana in the entire human library system, which led him to a large photo book called *Early Photography of the American West*. The first cameras had traveled west with the pioneers in the eighteen hundreds, and this book was filled with grainy black and white compositions of unsmiling pioneer families, bands of gold rush men, bleak scenes of wooden towns surrounded by mud, and smoky Native American villages.

<54>

Near the end of the book, there was a set of startling photographs. They were credited to a photographer named Archibald Wallace, and they depicted scenes of smoldering wreckage, buildings burned to the ground, with the occasional body among the debris. The photos were titled: *The Burning of Arcana, April 1868*. One month after the date on Selene's photo. Oliver had scoured the photos thoroughly, but there was no clue as to what might have happened, and no clue about Emalie either.

But there was something else in the book, on the page just before that series began. It was another photo credited to Mr. Wallace, and another fire event. This one was called: *Fire at the Arcana Hotel, New Years Day, 1868*. This photo was different than the later ones. Instead of being taken from a safe distance, as if Archibald had been standing in the middle of the road, this photo had been taken inside the ruined lobby of the hotel. Archibald would have had to crawl around and over the fallen beams and brick rubble to get inside.

The picture was aimed upward, focusing on the mostly ruined ceiling. Hanging from a still-intact beam was a glass chandelier, sparkling in smoky beams of sunlight. There was something about the angle of the composition, the photographer's natural instinct to get inside in spite of the danger, to look for the hidden detail, especially a chandelier....

Oliver couldn't be sure, but he had a feeling that Archibald Wallace hadn't take this photo. After all, there was another skilled photographer in Arcana at the time.

<55>

As he examined the photo for the tenth or maybe hundredth time, Oliver felt sure that Emalie had taken it. A postcard, not intentional, as she could never have known that it would end up in a photography book hundreds of years later, but still…. He rubbed his finger over the print.

"Oliver, supper!"

Oliver took another look at the photos of the smoking ruins of Arcana. Then, he slapped the book closed. He didn't like thinking about it.

Oliver, Phlox and Sebastian were silent through most of dinner, scraping forks against iron plates, munching their tiramisu and sipping from their goblets. Oliver sat there, feeling himself burning up, about Emalie at first, but then about his cohesion, and his powerlessness to stop it or anything else.

"How was work?" Phlox asked, looking warily across the table to Sebastian.

He sighed. "The usual. Lots of filing this time of year." Sebastian still worked for Half-Light, but he'd been demoted from the senior team that handled the Nexia Prophecy down to a clerical position filing legal briefs for the bureau of vampire housing, which acquired abandoned houses and buildings around the city and sold them to vampire families who wanted to build underneath. Oliver knew his dad hated it, but it wasn't worth saying any of that when their conversations were being monitored. "Get this, though," said Sebastian, "Malcolm was written up for filing late reports."

"Really?" Phlox almost smiled. "How the mighty

<56>

have fallen." Malcolm LeRoux was Lythia's father. He'd been in Half-Light's innermost circle, too; in fact, Lythia's brother Alexy had been the backup plan for the prophecy. But because Lythia had been conspiring with Dead Desiree, Malcolm had received even worse treatment than Sebastian: fired, and now he worked as a liaison to the human sewer department.

It almost made Oliver smile to think about that, but then not really. He figured that Lythia was probably having a pretty tough time at home, being the cause of her family's disgrace and all. And for as much as he hated her, Oliver knew that Lythia had been trying to save her younger brother, as Oliver had seen Bane try to do for him.

"How about you?" Sebastian asked Phlox.

"Thrilling," she said sarcastically. Phlox had also been punished: banished from the Central Council. She'd gotten a job as a hostess at *L'organo Sanguinante*, the classy restaurant in the Underground Center. "Well, we did have quite a dinner rush, and I did seat all the waiting families in perfect order," said Phlox proudly. This kind of organizing always pleased her. "But," she added bitterly, "they still look at me like I'm some kind of criminal." She scowled and dabbed her mouth with a napkin. "And school, Oliver?" she asked.

"Mmm," Oliver mumbled.

The only thing that made their nights bearable was that they were miserable together, wanting to stop the prophecy, yet making no progress.

<57>

Which made what Oliver had to report next difficult: "Carly got her demon tonight."

"Really?" said Phlox. "I didn't realize she'd started cohesion."

"She hadn't, until like, last week."

Sebastian shook his head. "That's not right. These cohesions are happening too fast."

"Some people say it's the media and today's culture," said Phlox. "Kids are growing up faster than they used to...."

"I don't know," said Sebastian, "There's got to be more to it than—"

"There's something else," said Oliver.

Phlox and Sebastian both turned to him. Their faces went blank, almost like they knew what was coming next.

Oliver swallowed hard, feeling a twist of nerves in his gut. "I had a cohesion dream."

"Your first...." Phlox began, but trailed off, glancing up at the ceiling.

"It's okay, mom, just say it. Yes!" Oliver shouted toward the ceiling, "I had my first real demon dream! Illisius is on his way. Happy?"

Sebastian reached over and patted Oliver's arm. "It could be some time yet."

"Years, even," added Phlox.

"Or any day now," muttered Oliver, "considering how fast it's happening to everyone else."

They each took another bite. Not so long ago, Oliver had lied about having had his first demon dream, and his

<58>

parents had been thrilled. Things had certainly changed.

"Well then," said Phlox in that high-pitched tone that indicated that she'd made up her mind about something, "I'll have to let your grandmother know. She'd slay me for not keeping her in the loop about such a big event in her grandson's life, even one like... this. Besides, they'll need to start preparing."

"For the end of the world," said Sebastian, sharing a serious gaze with Phlox.

They both turned to Oliver, their terse expressions focused on him. Oliver looked back. Here they were, and there was nothing that could be done.

"Let us know as the dreams progress," said Phlox.

"Okay," said Oliver. He felt his guts knot further. *The end of the world....*

They finished dinner in silence.

*　*　*

Friday night began uneventfully at school. Oliver found the same view out his window during cohesion: fog and starry water, a railing of some kind of steamship. It stayed that way through most of the cohesion session, but then, near the end, it changed.

The water began to solidify into true liquid, the stars vanishing. The fog started to lift. In the far distance, a land mass took shape. Oliver could make out a lighthouse, high bluffs behind it. Other lights on the hills to the south. Illisius' ship was arriving at a port, but the session ended before the ship docked.

<59>

Cohesion was exhausting, and Mr. VanWick took care to keep the sessions short. Still, Oliver wanted to stay longer. His insides were knotted with stress. He needed to know what he was seeing through the window, when it was, how close Illisius was to now.

No one else reported any change in their progress. Lythia, Theo and Maggots maintained their usual distance and animosity all through class.

At midnight, they went to Force Awareness and Manipulation with Ms. Nikkolai. They were working on floor-to-ceiling leaps, pushing against the forces in a move that looked somewhat like scaling a ladder made of thin air. It was levitation at a sprinter's pace. Oliver was getting better at it. The student having the hardest time was Lythia, who had once been able to do far more advanced skills with ease. Near the end of class, she vented her frustration by ordering Dean to break into the human's equipment closet, get a bag of baseballs, and hurl them at Oliver and Berthold, who were still on the ceiling at the time.

"Nice job avoiding my throws," said Dean as they headed back upstairs after class.

"Whatever," said Oliver, rubbing his shoulder; one of the baseballs had broken his collarbone, but it was healing up quickly, as vampire injuries did.

"I really hate being her minion," Dean muttered.

"At least she can't reach you over long distances anymore," said Oliver. This was another benefit of Lythia no longer having her demon: she could only control Dean when she was within sight of him. For this reason, they'd

<60>

changed out of their uniforms slowly so that they'd be last heading back upstairs.

They reached the first floor and passed the cafeteria, where the younger students were having lunch. In eighth Pentath, you could spend lunch anywhere on the school property. Lythia and the boys could usually be found out atop the basketball hoops in the back, so Oliver and Dean headed toward the front steps.

They were coming up a flight of stairs awash in grotesqua—here, the luminous, neon forms were a leering pack of hellhounds that lunged out at passers-by—just as a group of seventh graders was descending the flight above. The group reached the front doors ahead of Oliver and Dean. Three girls and a boy, all huddled tight, their heads close, whispering importantly.

Oliver didn't really mean to listen in on their conversation, but then he heard the words "the Legion" as the group headed outside. The last boy looked warily over his shoulder, as if making sure that they were alone. Oliver leaned against the wall, pushing Dean back, so that they were lost in the grotesqua.

"What's up?" Dean whispered.

"The Legion. That's what Lythia and Theo were talking about. Come on."

They crept to the front door. Dean caught the door just before it closed and pushed it slightly ajar. Oliver spectralized and climbed up the door frame, sliding out onto the brick wall outside.

The kids were huddled just around the corner from

<61>

the stairs, hidden from any teachers' view. Oliver scurried across the wall and then crept down until he was about ten feet above their heads.

They stood in a tight circle, each holding an identical object: A thin glass vial with a clear bulb at the top the size of a tennis ball. The glass was shaped to perfectly surround a single flower. Oliver recognized it: a moonflower, ghostly white with a pale purple center. Its stem was immersed in a pale pink liquid. They only bloomed at night, and were fairly common as vampire decorations, but these glass vessels were usually enchanted so that the flower could be made to bloom on command.

"So, this means tomorrow night, right?" one of the girls said.

"Yeah, remember what Lythia said? The meeting is the night after the blooming."

"Where? Cal Anderson again?"

"No, at the end of the last meeting they said it would be at Pele's Lair."

"What time?"

"At four, same as always."

"Okay, let's meet at the west entrance to the clubs at 3:30. Plan?"

"Plan."

One of the girls spoke quietly: "Do you think this is it?"

"I don't know," replied one of the boys. "You heard about Carly...."

"Theo said that Nocturne is next. And if he is, then yeah, it might be time to—"

<62>

"Sshh! We shouldn't talk about it here. Come on, we should get back before Ms. Estreylla notices we're gone."

Oliver watched them go, then dropped down to the ground and headed inside to relay the information to Dean.

Later that night, they discussed it while riding atop a bus to Dean's house. "So," said Dean, "Lythia has organized some kind of secret club?"

"A Legion," said Oliver somewhat sarcastically. "Theo and Maggots must be in it, too."

"And it has something to do with the cohesions. And you. Like with your destiny."

Oliver shrugged. "Knowing Lythia, it's some kind of scheme. Maybe she and Theo are trying to get their demons sooner. I could totally see them manipulating the younger kids somehow, like for some spell or something. She'd do anything to get another demon."

"If she does, she'll be able to control me again," said Dean.

"Yeah, and then, I don't know, maybe she wants to try to take over my destiny again, or something."

"But there's no way to do that."

"I know," said Oliver. He felt like there must be more to it than that, but he had no idea what. "I guess we could spy on their meeting."

"Ha." Dean clicked his tongue. "Sounds like old times. Emalie would approve."

"Yeah," said Oliver with a sigh. It wasn't much, but at least it was something. "Let's do it."

<63>

Chapter 6

THINGS TO DO
ON THE EVE OF THE END

Oliver and Dean transferred buses to get to Dean's house. It was a cool, clear night, the wind laced with a salty smell of the ocean.

"The Legion meets tomorrow night. So, what should we do tonight?" Dean asked glumly.

"I don't know," Oliver replied. The brief feeling of optimism about spying on the legion had worn off, and Oliver was back to thinking about cohesion, about the end, about the two years, over seven hundred and fifty days, all spent with nothing from Emalie. "Who cares?" he spat. "Everything sucks."

"We could hit the movies."

Oliver huffed. "What's the point? Of anything? If we sit around watching a movie, we're not doing anything to stop the prophecy, but there's nothing to do to stop the prophecy, so it's like, whatever." He threw up his hands.

<64>

"Nothing matters." It was a feeling he couldn't help sinking into lately.

"Yeah," Dean sighed in agreement. "Well, I still have that bag. You know, in the freezer...."

Oliver shrugged. They'd had a funny idea recently, something dumb and gross and maybe even a little mean, but... "Sure," said Oliver. "Why not?" At least Bane would have approved.

"I gotta grab some dinner first though," said Dean, "I'm starving." As he said it, his voice seemed to lower a notch, as if the real creature inside him was surfacing.

They leapt off and walked through the sleepy three A.M. streets until they reached the one house with light glowing in its windows, albeit it around the edges of dark velvet curtains.

Inside, Dean's mom Tammy was lying on the couch, asleep in the blue light of the television. She sat up with a start, "Oh, hey guys." She got up quickly, tightening her robe and shuffling to the kitchen. "Just dozed off for a sec."

"No worries, mom," said Dean. "We can get dinner. It's okay."

"Nah, it's fine," said Tammy, yawning as she turned on the kitchen light and pulled a foil-covered dish from one of two refrigerators, this one for the undead food. She slid the tray onto the counter then got out a glass pitcher of blood. "We still have a bunch of stuff from the butcher co-op," she said, uncovering the dish of raw pig entrails soaked in lime juice, cayenne and cilantro. She glanced at

<65>

Dean. "Do you think this will be… enough?" She asked uncertainly.

"It's fine, mom, don't worry," Dean replied sulkily. "Everybody's brains are safe."

"That's not how I meant it, honey, I just—"

Dean waved his hand. "Nah, I know. It's cool." He didn't sound like it was.

"You know," said Tammy, sounding like she was forcing herself back into her old peppy tone, "I think another guy who comes to the community cuttings at the butcher shop may have an undead family member, too. I used to be the only one interested in taking the entrails home, but now he wants some. People think we're part of some weird culinary trend from L.A. or somethingggg-yah." Tammy was interrupted by a big yawn. "Excuse me. Okay, help yourself. I'll clean up and then it's back to bed for this old lady."

Dean grabbed a plate from the cabinets and handed Oliver a goblet. They were quiet as they got their food and ate it at the counter bar. Tammy bustled around, pink rubber gloves on, bleaching down the counter where the tray had been.

These days, she didn't stay up with Dean the way she used to. Dean's younger sister Elizabeth was now in 7th grade and on the school volleyball team. She had games and practices, so as it was, Tammy was leaving work early to make those events. Elizabeth was technically Dean's age now, or the age he'd been when he died. She was as tall as him. And she never got up during the night. Really,

<66>

the two didn't see all that much of each other. In the past, she'd always made her displeasure with Dean's condition known, but at least she'd been around. Oliver was pretty sure Dean missed seeing her, but he didn't talk about it.

Mitch had gotten laid off his night job, and had to go back to working days. He didn't get up much in the evening, either. Most of the times that Oliver came over, he and Dean were on their own.

"Okay," Tammy sighed, pulling off her gloves. "You guys have a good rest of the ni—Oh, honey!"

"What?" said Dean.

Oliver saw Tammy's gaping expression and followed the path of her eyes down to Dean's left leg. There was a huge blotchy stain on his jeans below his knee, and a pool of black liquid spreading on the floor around his foot.

"Oh, great," Dean moaned.

"It's okay," said Tammy, rummaging through a cabinet drawer and producing a pile of old, stained towels. She dropped to the floor and quickly started mopping up the mess.

Oliver's nose wrinkled at a smell like rancid meat and wet cinders.

"Did you bang your knee or anything?" Tammy was asking, her voice thick as she tried to inhale as little of the noxious fumes as possible.

"No, Mom," Dean said, his voice edgy with frustration. "All I did was the normal school stuff. Ugh, this sucks!" he shouted, a menacing snarl creeping into his voice, and he slapped his plate off the counter. It smashed against

<67>

the wall. Oliver couldn't help thinking of the sounds and actions of real zombies.

"Honey, it's okay, it's okay," Tammy said. "It will be fine." Oliver thought it sounded like she was trying to convince herself as much as Dean. "Here, just... sit down and I'll get the sewing kit and bandages. We'll see if we can patch that leg up." Tammy spun to the cabinets again as Dean slouched into a seat. "You're sure you didn't do anything excessive at school?"

"Mom, no!" snapped Dean. "It's just this stupid... me!"

"Hey, Oliver," a groggy voice said from across the room. Kyle had come down, in his pajamas, hair sticking this way and that. He was ten now, and though he still liked hanging out with Dean and Oliver, Tammy kept him on a strict time limit so he wasn't too tired for school, soccer, and guitar lessons.

"Ky just hold on—" Tammy began, but Kyle rounded the table and saw Dean's leg, his jeans rolled up, and the long, wide tear in his yellow skin, chunky black fluid oozing out.

"Oh gross! What happened?"

"Nothing," Dean muttered.

Kyle slapped his hands over his nose. "It reeks!"

"Shut up!" Dean snapped and pushed him. He probably meant it like any annoyed older brother, but the force sent Kyle careening back across the room.

Oliver leapt off his stool, arcing through the air and catching Kyle before he smashed into the dining room

<68>

table. With the force of Dean's push, he'd probably have broken a few bones.

"Ow," Kyle groaned, clutching his chest, the wind knocked from him.

"Oh, I— sorry...." Dean stammered. Oliver gazed at him, saw the wide eyes and how Dean's face fell as he realized what he'd just done. And Oliver felt his insides sink, too, weighed down by a guilty feeling he often had, because, just like the impending end of the world, Dean's condition was his fault, too.

Tammy sniffed and wiped at her eyes as she gazed from Kyle back to Dean.

"Hey," Oliver said quickly to Kyle, "wanna go out back and practice?"

Kyle nodded. "Yeah." Oliver hurried him past Dean and Tammy and through the kitchen.

"Wear shoes!" Tammy called as they reached the back door. Kyle slipped on his sneakers and they headed out into the small grass backyard.

When Oliver closed the door, Kyle glanced back at the house and his face grew serious. "He's getting bad."

"It looks worse than it is, I think," said Oliver, but he wasn't sure if he meant it.

Kyle nodded, but frowned. "I put a padlock on the inside of my door," he said. "Elizabeth, too. Dad helped us set them up. And Mom and Dad both sleep with axes under their beds." Kyle looked at the ground. "He doesn't know any of that."

Oliver nodded. "He's still your brother."

<69>

"But not for much longer." Kyle looked up at Oliver. He was up to Oliver's chin now, but he still had child's eyes, big, searching, scared. "I mean… right?"

Oliver didn't know how to respond.

Kyle headed over to the shed and grabbed four long, straight sticks, former broom handles, that were leaning against the door. Kyle was fascinated with vampire stuff in general, but whereas he'd once been into the gross-out stories and toys like dismemberment dolls, now he had older tastes, like this method of two-stick martial arts, called Eskrima.

Oliver held his two rattan sticks in a ready position.

Kyle faced him a few feet away. He spun to attack, one stick horizontal for blocking, one twirling over his head.

Oliver dodged and blocked. The two danced around the yard, sticks spinning, until finally, Oliver undercut Kyle's legs and sent him falling on his backside.

He held out his hand and helped Kyle up. "Good moves."

"Thanks," said Kyle.

"Hey guys." Dean came outside. He had new jeans on and was wearing a long wool coat. "How was the sparring?" He sounded more like himself again.

"Good," said Oliver. "He gets better all the time. How's your leg?"

"Stupid, pathetic, crappy," muttered Dean. He looked at Kyle. "Sorry about pushing you."

"It's okay," Kyle replied, but he was looking away.

"Mom says it's time for bed," said Dean. He turned

<70>

to Oliver and held up a plastic grocery bag sagging with small heavy objects. "Still wanna go?"

Oliver shrugged. "Sure," he said, thinking, *why not?* It would be funny, and at least it was something to do. "Later, Kyle."

"Bye," Kyle said quietly, eyeing the bag in Dean's hand with a frown.

Oliver and Dean circled around the house and headed downtown.

"Thanks for playing with Kyle," said Dean.

"No worries," said Oliver.

"He was the only member of the family that wanted me around at this point, but, maybe not anymore."

"Come on, that's not true," said Oliver, but Dean might have been right. And it was unfair and it sucked. *Another reason to open that Gate*, he thought darkly. Except opening the Gate would kill Kyle, Dean's family, even Dean... Ugh! Every thought he had lately was dark and terrible and hopeless. Really, what was even the point of this existence? What was the point of anything they did when it was all going to end in destruction and death, at any moment?

Oliver felt like he could barely stand being in his own head. Even just getting through the night felt impossible. Everything felt heavy, crushing, like he had to try to not think about anything just to endure each moment.

Which made what they were about to do with that bag in Dean's hand all the more appropriate. A distraction. From everything. All the everything that didn't even matter and yet crushed him anyway.

<71>

"How many do you have?" Oliver asked as they jumped off the bus near Seattle Center.

Dean patted his bulky coat, the bag hidden inside. "Five, I think."

They walked a little ways and entered a Kid Valley burger restaurant. It was open late and bustling with a mix of vampires (here for the unadvertised blood milk shakes and French fries), assorted other demons who couldn't get enough of fast food (and who also didn't have to worry about cholesterol or trans fats), and humans: mostly groups of teens, some older. Many of the humans were noticeably intoxicated. Oliver and Dean slipped into a booth by the window.

Dean surveyed the crowd, then nodded across the room. "How about them?"

Oliver glanced over and saw a booth full of teenagers giggling and stuffing their faces. "Perfect," said Oliver, watching the happy little scene. He felt like he hated them. Not in the traditional way—vampires tended to look down on humans as primitive creatures—but more because they were so happy, so oblivious to their own peril. Not just to Oliver's world-ending destiny, but even to the demons around them right now. These humans were such frail little things, yet it was like they thought they were invincible.

Or maybe Oliver was just jealous. He remembered times with Emalie and Dean, out late, sitting around laughing, thinking the world was theirs... but that was a long time ago now, so long ago it was almost like it had never happened.

<72>

"Here we go." Dean produced the bag and slipped his hand inside. He pulled something out in a closed fist and handed it to Oliver beneath the table. Oliver took the cold object and slid it into his sweatshirt pocket. He nodded to Dean and left the booth.

As he approached the humans, he spectralized and stopped just beside the booth. The five kids were wrapped up in a laugh-filled conversation about their evening's misadventures. The girl closest to him, with dyed blonde hair and wearing a Ballard High sweatshirt, was leaning toward the boy diagonally across from her. A tall burger lay on her tray, only a first bite taken. Perfect.

Just do it. Who cares anyway. Don't be a lamb.

As the girl talked busily, Oliver's transparent hand flashed out. The girl sensed something and turned, but Oliver was already gone, circling back toward his booth.

He reappeared as he sat down. "Mission accomplished," he said to Dean.

Dean turned to watch the girl with the closest thing he'd had to a smile all day. "Nice. Here we go..."

Oliver watched as the girl continued talking. He sensed his nerves squirming inside, and couldn't help feeling a little bit bad about what was about to happen. *Whatever!* He reminded himself. It didn't matter. Nothing mattered. Soon this girl would be gone, just like this restaurant, this air, everything. Nothing mattered, so why not have some fun?

The girl picked up the sandwich absently and took a bite. Her teeth sank through the soft bun... then suddenly crunched against something hard. She flinched, grimacing,

<73>

and pulled the sandwich from her mouth.

The frozen rat's head fell free, thudding on her tray.

Her shrieking scream tore through the room. The whole restaurant turned. Dean exploded with laughter. Oliver smiled, too. It was something to see: the whole table jumping up in a single spasm, the girl slapping at her mouth, the tough-looking crowd of teen vampires nearby pointing and laughing, the girl sprinting for the door in shrieks and tears. And yet...

She would think this was awful, too, Oliver thought. But whatever! Emalie wasn't here. She was never here, anymore. So who cared?

We do.

Oliver felt himself yanked backward, as if through the plastic booth itself, and the world suddenly washed away into gray.

There was a burst of pale light, and he found himself standing on the gray, boulder-strewn beach of the Shoals, Jenette's hands on his shoulders.

She stepped around him, to where the restaurant was still visible through a filmy window, though the sound of it was gone, and she grabbed Dean and dragged him through as well.

Guh! Dean exclaimed as he toppled back to the sand.

Jenette darted around and stood before them, arms crossed. Here in the Shoals, something like her former human self was visible: a small delicate face and long chestnut hair that reached almost to her waist, the white flannel pajamas with tiny smiling frogs on them that she'd

<74>

been wearing on the night she'd died in a house fire. While her facial features were still human like, she no longer had eyes exactly, but rather smoky hollows where eyes would be. Still, it was easy enough to decipher the meaning of the glare she was aiming at Oliver and Dean.

That was awful what you were doing!

What's the big deal? Oliver snapped back. *We're just having some fun.*

That's not fun. It's cruel!

Whatever! That girl will be fine, and even if she's not, who cares? My cohesion's started! She'll be dead in a few weeks! Everybody will be! It doesn't matter.

It does to him. Jenette nodded over their shoulders. Oliver turned to see Nathan hovering at the edge of the inky black water, stars glowing beneath its depths. He had his back to them, slinging stones out across the calm sea, each skip making rings. *And,* Jenette added, *it matters to me, too.*

Oliver threw up his hands. *Great. You guys are like having a second set of parents!*

Why, because we care about you? snapped Jenette. *We're supposed to be trying to save the world and you're acting like—*

Like it's going to end, I know! Oliver couldn't help shouting. *I should know, I'm the one who's going to end it!*

Oliver—

But Oliver couldn't take it anymore. *No, Jenette. Illisius is coming. Any day now. It's OVER. There's no*

<75>

magic Triad, no Emalie, no nothing! Oliver hated saying these things, but it also felt like some kind of terrible relief. To shout out the black thoughts he'd been keeping inside. *So, guess what?* he went on, *I'm a freakin' vampire. He's a zombie. At least let us have some fun.* He started to step around her.

Where do you think you're going?

I'm going back. Get out of my—

Jenette's hands thrust out and energy burst into Oliver's chest, sending him soaring backward. He tumbled through the air and landed with a splash in the edge water. His shoulder cracked on a black boulder, sending a tremor of pain through his barely healed collar bone.

He lay there for a minute, dazed, staring up at the featureless gray sky, feeling the strange, lukewarm liquid seeping into his shirt. Then he felt a warmth spreading inside him. He looked up to see Nathan bending over and pulling him up by the arm. Oliver almost wanted to yank his arm away. He didn't even want to feel that warmth anymore, the sense of being whole that Nathan gave him, because it only made the truth worse, the awful truth—

When you do things like that, it makes me feel like our connection is fading, said Nathan.

Oliver looked away and shrugged. *It's going to.*

It's not over yet, said Nathan. *And if you act like it is, then they've already won.*

Nathan sat down on the sand, arms around his knees. Oliver crawled over and sat beside him. His clothes were dripping wet but he didn't really feel it, as this water was

<76>

more energy than liquid. His feet were still in the lapping breakwater. It made little white sparks when it touched him.

We have to keep up hope, said Nathan. Here in the Shoals, his facial features were visible, and he looked almost like Oliver's twin.

Oliver huffed to himself. With Nathan beside him, he could feel that resolve, that hope, returning. It was like the opposite of what he'd been feeling since the first cohesion dream, almost like Nathan and Illisius were opposites. Made sense, he guessed: a soul and a demon.

And with that warmth, he could see how Nathan was right. There was still time. *But....* Oliver threw up his hands. *I have no idea what else we can do.*

Nathan shrugged. *Yeah. That makes two of us.*

There was a plunk in the water. Dean had started skipping rocks. *Hey Nathan, want a shot at the record?*

Nathan stood up. *You mean my record?* Nathan was perhaps the greatest rock skipper in this world. He'd had plenty of time to practice, as he'd spent most of Oliver's existence here at the Shoals.

Not for long, said Dean.

Nathan got up, leaving Oliver with a shuddering cold feeling. He pulled his knees up, wrapped his arms around them. His anger had soured to guilt. It wasn't any better.

Jenette came and sat down beside him. *Sorry,* said Oliver.

It's okay. I mean, I get it.

Oliver nodded. *Have you been to see your mom lately?*

No, said Jenette. Her voice tightened. *She's getting*

<77>

worse. It doesn't do any good, me going there, if I'm just going to scare her. Still, I might try again soon. She glanced up the beach. *Some of the other wraiths have started visiting their loved ones and saying goodbye, too, you know, in case we go.* Oliver followed her gaze and saw the other wraiths standing here and there. They all looked human here, at least somewhat, and stood, barefoot, most gazing out to sea.

Oliver knew that the wraiths would survive the opening of the Gate, though their grief would likely intensify, as the humans they loved would be destroyed. This only made Oliver feel another wave of guilt. Still more beings whose fates were tied to his destiny.

That must suck, said Oliver.

Yeah, but... there's another way for a wraith, Jenette said quietly. *I've been thinking about it a lot lately.*

What's that?

Well, a wraith can free itself from earth. Become energy, like a freed soul... if they find someone to take their grief.

What does that mean?

Someone absorbs the wraith's grief as part of their own. They become responsible for it.

How do you get someone to do that? Oliver asked.

There's an enchantment, said Jenette. *And also, I have to invite the person. My grief is mine to give.* Jenette sighed. *But it's tough. Nobody wants more grief, you know? Everyone already has enough of their own sadness to bear.*

Yeah, I guess, Oliver agreed. On a night like tonight,

<78>

he couldn't imagine having to manage someone else's grief, too.

I chose someone anyway, though, said Jenette, and the thought seemed to lift her spirits. *I did the ritual and everything… but I haven't asked them yet.*

Oh. Oliver wondered if she'd tell him who it was. He thought about asking.

But then she said, *You know what else is neat?*

What?

Grief is powerful. The person who takes on a wraith's grief can use it.

Yeah, what for?

It has the power that all grief has, to bind things together. The same power that traps a wraith here. There's an incantation and everything. It's pretty cool.

Huh, said Oliver. That was pretty cool, and he could think of one person he would like to bind to himself, or at least to this time and space….

The view of the beach flickered around them.

Time to go, said Jenette with a sigh. It took a lot of energy for the wraiths to hold Oliver and Dean here. *Too soon, as usual. Oliver, promise me you won't just go back and start terrorizing humans again. Promise me you'll keep trying to have hope.*

Oliver stood. *All right, I promise. But I don't know how that's going to help. It's not like anything we've tried has worked.*

Well, maybe something will come along when you least expect it.

Yeah. Oliver turned. *Dean, let's go.*

<79>

See ya, said Nathan.

Sure. Oliver didn't want to say what he was thinking, which was: *hope so.* Because would he? Was there still time? When Illisius arrived, that would be that. Oliver would get his demon, and he and Nathan would be separated. Nathan would be freed into energy, his warmth gone forever.

They headed back up the beach to the round window where the Kid Valley was visible, and Jenette pushed them through. They returned to their booth in the busy restaurant.

"Okay, well," said Dean, "Now what do we—" but he didn't finish.

There was someone sitting across from them.

"HELLO, MR. NOCTURNE. MR. AUNDERS." The man sitting on the other side of the booth was tall, with neat black hair and a black suit. He looked at them blankly with eyes that were solid black, no iris or pupil. And he had no mouth, just smooth alabaster skin. The voice was coming from a speaker, a copper box with a round wire mesh center. It protruded from the man's chest, through a neat hole in his clothes.

"AEONIAN PARCEL SERVICES WOULD LIKE TO INFORM YOU THAT WE HAVE A PACKAGE DELIVERY FOR YOU."

Dean spoke sideways to Oliver. "Um, what is this?"

"I don't know," Oliver replied, but he thought the company sounded familiar.

"TO ACCEPT DELIVERY, PLEASE TOUCH TWO FINGERS TO THE COUNTERSIGN ON YOUR INNER LEFT WRIST."

<80>

"The—" Oliver glanced down. His inner left wrist.... There was the small black tattoo of a leaf that Emalie had given him and Dean for transporting to and from the Delta, where they had met to plan in secret before Emalie left. Over the last two years, Oliver had pressed it any number of times and tried to close his eyes and travel there again, but it hadn't worked.

Oliver's head snapped up to Dean.

"Do you think?" asked Dean, his eyes wide like he was thinking it, too.

Oliver felt a burst of nerves, of hopeful fear. He held up two fingers to Dean. "Let's find out."

"To accept delivery, please t—"

Oliver placed two fingers on the tattoo and closed his eyes. There was a rush of wind and darkness.

<81>

Chapter 7

THE POST OFFICE
AT THE EDGE OF THE WORLD

When Oliver opened his eyes, he saw the fog-shrouded borderland of the Delta, where the black river Acheron flowed out of the world, delivering souls and energy into the universe beyond. He and Dean were standing on the high wooden platform, in the thick branches of an enormous tree where they'd once met with Emalie to plan. The river was far below, hidden beneath the canopy of a lush rainforest. Strange birds and creatures called through the perpetual folds of mist. Here and there, other giant trees sprouted up through the jungle and atop these were more platforms, orange fires glowing, indicating secret meetings in progress.

Oliver instinctively looked around, but their fire was out, the platform empty—

Except for a giant winged creature. It had charred, maroon skin and thick muscular legs that ended at pearl-

<82>

white talons, bat-like leathery wings, a wolf-like face, and giant yellow eyes.

It looked down at the two of them and screamed. "*Keeeeaaatchhhhhh!*"

"Um..." said Dean worriedly.

"PLEASE DON'T BE ALARMED."

Oliver spied another square copper box with a speaker implanted in the creature's chest. "THIS HERMESIAN DEMON IS HIGHLY TRAINED AND SKILLED AT ITS TASK. TO CONTINUE YOUR DELIVERY, PLEASE SAY 'OKAY.'"

"Okay," said Oliver.

The creature leaped into the air, beating its wings, and snatched Dean and Oliver, one in each giant claw.

"PLEASE HANG ON," advised the voice.

The creature vaulted upward and soared out over the forest. Mist left a cool film on Oliver's face. The creature's huge wing beats made it undulate up and down like a wave. It banked left and right to avoid the enormous trunks of the towering meeting trees. Oliver watched the forest canopy blur by below, now and then catching a glimpse of movement and hearing the roars of the hidden creatures that fed on the river's souls.

All at once, the trees gave way to smooth rock. Below, Oliver could see Acheron, its dark waters striped by blurry luminescent spirits. The river was now hurtling through a shallow rock canyon. Ahead, it cascaded off a sheer cliff of black, volcanic basalt, into what seemed to be an infinite void below.

The Hermesian flew out over this abyss, then tucked

<83>

its wings and dropped into a completely vertical descent, shooting past the edge of the cliff, the smooth beginning of the falls, then down and down alongside the frothing spray. Below, Oliver could only see black and the flickering of stars, as if they were hurtling down into the universe itself, off the edge of the world completely.

Out of the corner of his eye, though, he noticed that the sheer black cliff face to either side of the raging falls was developed, crisscrossed by one wooden walkway after another. Orange magmalights were strung along the railings, illuminating doors of varying sizes that were carved into the rock, each with a gleaming gold handle. There were doors stretching up and down and in either direction: thousands, maybe tens of thousands.

The creature flapped its wings viciously and they came to a hovering halt. Oliver craned his neck to see up. The top of the waterfall was no longer even visible.

The demon placed Oliver and Dean, standing, onto one of the walkways. With a screech, it soared away.

The walkway creaked beneath their feet.

"Whoa," breathed Dean, peering through the gaps in the damp boards.

"MR. NOCTURNE, MR. AUNDERS, WELCOME."

Standing in front of them was a short creature, just over half their height, with four arms and four legs, more arachnid than humanoid, its body coated in black fur that glistened with droplets from the falls. It had clusters of eyes, pink in color, eight pupils on each side, grouped together and yet seeming to rotate independently, taking in

<84>

all directions at once. It stepped closer, its claws clacking on the walkway, looking potentially sinister in the dim orange light. Oliver heard a similar sound, and with a quick glance around saw that more of these creatures were patrolling the walkways above and below, and scaling the walls in between.

The creature hissed thinly at Oliver and Dean, and then spoke in that same voice, from an identical copper transmitter box implanted just below its neck. "WE WERE INSTRUCTED BY OUR CLIENT TO BRING YOU HERE ON THIS EXACT EVENING."

"Who's your client?" Oliver asked anxiously.

"THE LOCK HAS BEEN DESIGNED TO OPEN WITH YOUR COUNTERSIGN," the voice continued, one of the arachnid creature's hands sweeping toward the stone door beside them. "JUST PRESS IT TO THE HANDLE TO ENTER. WHEN YOU ARE FINISHED, PLEASE PLACE ALL CONTENTS INTO THE CENTRAL FLAME. ANY QUESTIONS?"

"Um, yeah," said Oliver, looking around. "Where are we, exactly?"

"GENERALLY SPEAKING, YOU ARE AT MW83705 EXIT CATARACT 3. SPECIFICALLY, YOU ARE AT BOX 6022 OF YOUR NEAREST AEONIAN PARCEL SERVICES RETAIL LOCATION. NOW, IF YOU'LL EXCUSE ME...." The creature turned and scaled the wall, heading diagonally away to where a Hermesian demon was delivering another customer to a walkway above.

Dean's neck was craning up and down. "Was that supposed to make sense?"

<85>

"Yeah," said Oliver. He knew the references from school. "MW means 'middle world.' I think, on a multi-world map, Earth is called middle world 83705."

"One world of eighty three thousand," Dean mused.

"Those are only the middle worlds," said Oliver. "There are upper and lower, too, but it's hard to keep count of those because they're not made of matter, just energy, so they're always bleeding together and splitting off and stuff."

Dean shook his head. "Basically what you're saying is the universe is really big."

"Yeah." Oliver turned to the wall. "And here on the edge of the borderland would be a good place for getting your mail if you were, like, some kind of multi-world demon."

"Demons get snail mail?" asked Dean.

"Well, but it's not like real mail, I mean, like we think of it. It's not like, paper and envelopes and stuff."

"Okay," said Dean. He looked over Oliver's shoulder. "Wow."

Oliver turned to look back at the enormous waterfall. It was the width of a skyscraper at least, a mix of shimmering energy and foam, falling from mists of distance above down into starry darkness. But along the way, now and then, feathers of pale luminous, greenish-tinted light peeled off, drifting into space and dissipating.

"Souls," said Oliver, watching them go. "Energy into the universe."

"They made it through the delta," said Dean, "and now they're home free."

<86>

One of the Hermesians swooped by and snatched a soul from the air, sucking it down.

"Or not," Dean added.

Oliver looked down at the tattoo. His feeling of anticipation grew.... He turned back to the door. "Let's go in." He pressed his wrist to the cool gold door handle. There was a loud grinding, like of stone bolts sliding. The door swung inward.

Oliver and Dean stepped from the damp, dark cliff face into a warm, fire-lit room. It was small, the walls made of rock, the ceiling barely above their heads. The flame burned in a metal bowl suspended by chains in the center of the room. The door shut behind them, cutting off the roar of the falls. All that remained was the crackle of the fire and the scuffing of their feet on the stone floor.

"Feels like a tomb," said Oliver.

At the back wall was a small cylindrical pedestal holding up a long, thick stone table that looked more like a box. Actually, it resembled a coffin, except that it seemed to be solid stone. It did have a big brass padlock on it, but there was something lying atop it that was much more important. Oliver's steps quickened. He reached out and grabbed the object.

"I thought you said it wasn't, like, snail mail," said Dean, arriving beside him.

Oliver looked at the paper object in his hand.

An envelope. Rectangular and white, but discolored by smudges of grime. The surface was crinkled, the edges browned and torn. In the top right was a faded stamp of

<87>

blue ink, the print barely legible. Oliver could just make some of it out: *Ma— 1868*. Probably March....

"Is it—" Dean began.

"Yeah," said Oliver, because the handwriting in the center was unmistakable:

For Oliver and Dean

-e

The seam was sealed with a blot of red wax, marked with the impression of a scarab beetle. Oliver slipped his finger beneath the corner and tore open the letter. He pulled out a folded sheet of cream-colored paper, and as he did so, his sensitive vampire nose detected the faintest scent, one he hadn't known for two years, and it made him tremble.

He unfolded the paper, trying to be careful but trying to go fast, fingers shaking, and saw that it was full from edge to edge with handwriting. In the top corner:

Dear Oliver and Dean,

It was really her! Emalie....

"Something's happening," reported Dean.

Before Oliver could even begin to read further, light grew and gathered around them. He looked up to see the world swimming out of focus. Light overwhelmed everything, and then dissolved into shimmering white.

Oliver felt a moment of pure weightlessness, and then his feet touched solid, uneven ground. He blinked hard. The light faded; the wind died down. Oliver began to make out a form, a figure, standing before them. And he heard a voice he'd waited forever to hear:

"Hey guys."

<88>

Chapter 8

THE LETTER

She stood there before them and Oliver thought that she looked like she always had, like she always did in his mind, with her wide, dark eyes, her brown hair in two braids, her cute, curvy nose, high cheeks, a camera slung around her neck... except she was wearing a hand-sewn white shirt with a high collar, a dark gray ruffled skirt and scuffed tan cowboy boots. And instead of her usual camera, she was lugging a bulky black box model on a leather strap over her shoulder. Its wooden tripod was slung across her back, almost like a weapon.

Oliver looked around and saw that they were standing in the middle of a dirt street, rickety board buildings on either side, along a warped walkway. There were horses tied to hitches. A stagecoach parked in the distance. The sun was high and bright in a clear blue sky. The air smelled like sweet sweat and sour manure, felt light and dry, chalky with dust and desert.

<89>

A loud whistle sounded from behind them. Oliver turned to see that the road ended at the steps to a long wooden train platform with a small brick station house. A black steam engine pulled in, belching big clouds of smoke. The name Central Pacific Railroad was on the engine's side.

Arcana! They were here.

He turned back to Emalie. She was standing there, smiling. "Hi," said Oliver, but the word came out hoarse, weak, and he wanted to say it again but then didn't want to sound like a moron and she'd probably heard him but still he felt like an idiot.

"Hey, cuz," said Dean.

Looking at her, Oliver wondered: did she look different? Taller? Older? It had been two years... yet he thought she maybe looked the same. It was hard to tell.

But never mind that. Oliver felt his feet and fingers tingling. *Do it!* He shouted at himself. *Do what you've been wishing you did for two years!* And yet he kept standing there like his feet were impaled in the ground with railroad spikes. *Come on, you idiot!*

Because, honestly, how many times had he relived that last night in his mind? Relived Emalie saying goodbye and rushing up and kissing him as he just stood there and then she was gone and why hadn't he thrown his arms around her and kissed her back or anything and now, NOW was his chance and he was just standing there and so NO, he was not just going to let this moment pass by.

He stepped to Emalie. "I missed you," he said aloud,

<90>

thinking, *yes!*, that was what he wanted her to know! And he threw his arms around her, to hug her first, and then—

But his arms went right through her.

"What—" Oliver began.

"Welcome to Arcana," Emalie said, talking right over him.

Oliver stepped back. He waved a hand through Emalie again.

Of course.

For as real as Emalie had seemed on first glance, this wasn't actually her. She was part of the letter, and the letter was an enchantment, like a program. Oliver looked around at Arcana again. The effect was impressive. Everything seemed almost real, but maybe not quite, like things were flickering at their edges.

Despite that, Emalie held up her hands almost like she was doing her old trick of reading Oliver's thoughts. "I know, right?" she said. "Not bad, Emalie, not bad. I practiced this enchantment for months before I wrote this letter. Can you smell the manure? Gross, right? I never thought I'd get used to it, but—well, come on, we don't have much time. The enchantment can only hold so much information." Emalie turned and started walking, putting out her arms like she was going to throw one around each of them, but they just passed right through Oliver and Dean as she walked up the street like a tour guide.

Oliver fell into step behind her, but inside he felt himself deflating. This was good, he guessed, better than nothing. To finally hear from her, to see her sort-of, but, still....

<91>

"It's pretty fun living here," Emalie went on as they walked. She held up the giant, clunky black camera. "I've been interning with the town photographer, Archie. These cameras are so old-school, and the darkroom, super primitive, but that kinda makes the results pretty great. The negatives that we make are on these big plates of glass, coated in silver dust. Seriously, old photography is as amazing as any enchantment. And, it's a nice break from my studies. Get to be on my own a bit, though I know the Orani Circle is monitoring me whenever I'm out of their sight."

"I know that feeling," said Oliver.

Emalie spoke right over him. "Ooh, and check that out."

She pointed across the street, to the charred lumber and piles of brick. Oliver recognized it from the photo he'd seen of the burned Arcana Hotel. "That place totally burned to the ground last week, and Archie let me go and get the shots. It was so cool."

"That's so her," Dean commented.

"I bet you're saying that's so *me*, right?" said the Emalie guide.

"Ha," said Dean.

Oliver didn't say anything. He couldn't stop staring at this image of Emalie and feeling frustrated, almost... angry. Sure, this was something, and he was glad to see her, but it wasn't the real her. He wondered if, in a way, this maybe felt worse than not seeing her at all.

A horse-drawn cart rumbled down the rutted street,

<92>

spraying dust. Oliver and Dean instinctively jumped out of the way, but then Dean reached out and stuck a hand through the cart's side as it passed. "No worries," he said.

"Over there is the apothecary that my mom and Aunt Kathleen have been running," said Emalie. "You know, to earn our keep in town. We sell herbal remedies and advice and stuff."

"Sounds like Desiree," Oliver muttered, knowing Emalie couldn't hear him.

"I work a couple shifts there during the week," tour guide Emalie continued. "It's cool 'cause I don't have to go to school. There's a schoolhouse, but it's only for kids through age ten. After that, you're expected to work with your family. Or go get a job at the gold mine. So I get to do my thing."

The town buildings ended abruptly and the road forked in three directions. Emalie turned and followed the one that curved up a hill into tall pine trees, their trunks covered in thick, crusty orange bark. The shade was cool, sweet smelling. The deep ruts in the dirt road were filled with soft yellow pine needles, making their footfalls quiet. The space in between the trees was carpeted in tall, pale blonde grass.

"Really, it's been kinda like being at summer camp," said the Emalie guide. "It's amazing what you take for granted until it's gone. I mean, no electricity; we live by lantern, but it's cool how dark it is when it gets dark. Like, outer space dark. And gardening is this whole big thing that takes hours, not to mention milking the cows

<93>

and goats, and you know, chickens don't kill and clean themselves.... I'm actually pretty good at that part. We have an enchantment to kind of calm them, so it's easier."

Oliver thought of the stilling gaze he performed, of Emalie calming chickens before killing, and felt another yearning connection to her that soured to frustration.

"And here we are." Emalie crested a rise and paused. Ahead was a wide, gently sloping clearing, crisscrossed by split rail fences that separated pastures and gardens. The road ended at a large white farmhouse. Beyond that was a big barn made of gray, unpainted boards, a few horses tied outside, and past that was a circular wooden building, or more accurately it had about twenty sides, making it nearly circular, and a conical roof with an opening at the top. Smoke drifted from it.

Beneath the grunts and bleats of livestock, Oliver could hear the babbling of a stream from the far end of the stead. In the distance, a trio of tall mountains loomed, their tops holding a few last drifts of snow.

Oliver recognized the farmhouse, or at least its front steps, from the photo they'd seen in Selene's bedroom back in the Asylum Colony. Things were beginning to come together. And yet this reminded Oliver of what else he'd learned about Arcana.

"This is nice," said Dean.

Oliver turned to see him with his face upturned to the sun, his eyes closed. It was funny; Oliver hadn't even noticed that they were standing in daylight strong enough to slay him instantly. He'd been more concerned with

<94>

Emalie. He looked up at the brilliant orb. "Can't feel it."

"No, but just having to squint is nice," said Dean. He sighed. "I miss it." He looked down, holding out his bare arms with their ruined skin, and his face fell. The purple and tan blotches had become more like black and dark brown. A rift had opened by his elbow, dripping black, foamy fluid. Dean just shook his head.

Oliver turned back to the farm. "Where is everybody?" he asked aloud, forgetting that she couldn't hear him.

"The farm is in pretty good shape," said the Emalie guide, "considering we've only been here three months."

"Three months?" Oliver asked aloud.

"Dad's gotten into the daily routines with everybody. Kathleen goes fly fishing in the stream all the time. She's teaching me. We have an enchantment to call the fish. This way." Emalie started walking down the hill.

But Oliver didn't move.

"Come on," said Dean.

"No." He couldn't take it anymore. To see Emalie again but not see her, to be led along without his questions being answered. It was making him crazy!

Emalie stopped and turned. "Wait, yeah…. I should explain," she said, almost like she still knew what he was thinking. "I'm writing this letter as I go—there's no backspace button in 1868, you know?—and I just realized that I have to explain the whole time thing, don't I? That's probably bugging you, since you're getting this letter so much later." She made a sympathetic smile.

"Yes," said Oliver uselessly.

<95>

"Listen," Emalie continued. "At the time that I'm writing this letter, I've been here for a little over three months. We left in September, you remember, but when we arrived in Arcana, it was December. Time travel is funny like that. Anyway, now it's March 13, 1868. And you guys are probably worried about how Arcana gets destroyed in April, according to history, but remember, that history was written before we gathered all the Orani here. I have a great great grand cousin here named Aralene, who's crazy and honestly if we hadn't all showed up, I'd bet on her being the one who would've ended up causing the mass hysteria that supposedly destroyed this town, but none of that matters, because we're here now, so the future will be different. And besides, we'll be gone long before April."

"Okay," said Oliver. "But what about—"

"And I know what you're thinking.... You're reading this after over two years. I—" Her face grew serious, her mouth small. "I don't know what that's been like for you guys, but... it was necessary. We have news for you, and I had to wait to give it to you until you needed to know."

"Needed to know?" Oliver found himself nearly shouting. "What about needing to know that you were alive? Or that you were ever going to get in touch?" The Emalie guide just gazed at him blankly, almost like she knew to give him time to respond. "Why couldn't you have sent little notes," Oliver went on, "like, just to let us know that we'd hear from you at some point? Why—"

Emalie started speaking again. "I've heard your messages, the ones you sent with the wraiths. We pick

<96>

them up during our monitoring circle. They're sweet...."
Emalie trailed off and for a moment her face cracked, her
eyes seeming to grow. Oliver knew that face, and knew
that at least a little, she was missing him too. It helped to
see it, and calmed him down a little.

"Half-Light is monitoring you," said Emalie, "and
there are others out there, like Desiree, who could have
been listening. Could have traced any message I sent before
now..." Emalie looked back at the circular building. "I'm
sorry, you guys," she said. "I'm so sorry it's been so long,
but, like I said, now is the time, and I can't make this long,
so I have to show you what you need to know."

She started walking again.

"Come on," Dean said to Oliver, following her.

Oliver caught up and they walked past the farmhouse
to the circular building. They followed Emalie through the
open door.

There was a single large room inside, dark, candles
and incense burning around the walls. A circle of women
sat on the dirt floor, dressed in white robes, legs crossed,
wrists on their knees, palms up. Above them, filling the
high open space, was a massive model of orbiting spheres
and clouds. There were solid brass objects like planets, and
other nebulous shapes that glowed with luminous stars
inside them, almost like bubbles. There were hundreds,
and the sense of thousands more in the blurry distance,
like they were seeing just one small slice of the universe.
A map, Oliver figured. As the worlds spun, dotted lines
appeared and disappeared, momentarily connecting
worlds.

<97>

"This is the Orani circle," said Emalie. "The circle of Six, plus Selene and Phoebe—that's my mom, oh, and they call me Eos, which means dawn—and Aunt Kathleen's here too. Everyone's gathered here for safety, but also because of what's about to happen."

Oliver wanted to ask what, but remembered it was useless. He instead watched the orbiting worlds above, lines flickering between them.

"Those lines are connections," said Emalie. "Convergences, where worlds pass close enough to one another that their forces weave together and influence one another, and watch...."

The worlds kept spinning, dipping and diving in broad arcs, and then Oliver could see it starting to happen: a number of objects drifted into a line, and a new beam of light began to form in between them, a bright white, solid beam of energy connecting between the worlds. It was happening in other places in the model, too, things lining up, and many bursts of white light, lines connecting worlds like spider silk, at every angle, with all the lines converging in the center.

Oliver had seen this, a diagram of it, in his Multi-World Math book, the giant sphere of lines connecting in the middle, forming a star-like shape, and finally he remembered the familiar term, the one he'd heard recently, just as Emalie said it—

"A Great Radiance," said Emalie. "When the worlds line up, and the forces stream with minimum distance from one to the next, in toward Nexia. It's like a moment of

<98>

perfect universal balance, and it only happens once every thirty five thousand three hundred and sixty four years." Emalie shrugged. "Give or take a decade. During a Great Radiance, travel from one world to the next is simplest. And there's one happening just about a week from your current date. When it happens, Earth will be at its closest distance to Nexia."

"A week?" Oliver exclaimed. "So then what?" But based on the tightening in his gut, he was pretty sure that he already knew.

"That's when Illisius will summon you, well, us I mean. He can't bring us to Nexia before then; even he's not that strong."

"But," said Oliver, "you're there, in Arcana."

Emalie smiled, almost like she could hear him. "Don't worry, I know you're making your worried no-face right now," said Emalie. "We're coming back."

Oliver felt a surge of relief. "When?"

"We have a few more things to do. I shouldn't tell you too much; I know you're being questioned by Half-Light—but basically, we're preparing enchantments for when we go to Nexia. Not just you and me: all of us. I'm coming back to you, and the rest of the Orani are heading for Nexia. To fight."

"Okay..." said Oliver, "but what about—"

"But what about the Triad of Finity," said Emalie. "That's what you'll be wondering. Well, we're close to figuring that out, too, or at least, to figuring out where we can find the one who knows. By the time I come back, we'll know."

<99>

Emalie turned to them. "Okay, I'm at the end of the page and that's all the enchantment power I've got. So... I'll see you guys soon, okay? It's just going to be a few more days."

"Sounds good," said Dean.

"Yeah," said Oliver. He tried to smile, then remembered that it didn't matter because she couldn't see him anyway. And besides, he didn't want to smile. Despite all the other things he'd just heard, only one fact was dominating all the rest in his mind: One week. That was it. Then, the end. But, no, not just the end anymore. Emalie was coming back. Maybe there was still a chance....

"Bye guys." The vision of Arcana began to flicker. White light edged in from the borders.

Once again, Oliver found himself saying goodbye when Emalie couldn't hear him....

There was a flash and they were back in the stone chamber. Oliver blinked, then looked down at the letter. The words were gone, the weathered paper blank.

"That's so secret agent," said Dean with a chuckle.

Oliver tried to respond, but couldn't really. The whole experience had left him drained. Seeing her, knowing how close the end now was, but also just the frustration of not being able to reply to her, to really talk with her, touch her....

He looked around the long rectangular table now, and when he saw it was blank, he bent and looked around the sides. If he understood correctly, this letter had been sitting in this vault for over a hundred-and-fifty years,

<100>

sent here just after Emalie prepared it, and stored until its delivery date. Maybe she'd written others, and they were here somewhere, in an alcove, or a safe or something.

Oliver peered at the walls but they were smooth. He checked around the coffin-like table. It did seem to have a lip, almost like it was in fact a box of some kind. Oliver pulled up on this edge, but the thick padlock held tight.

"Let's go," he muttered. He turned and crossed the room, tossing the letter into the fire bowl, where it curled into a black fist. He yanked open the door and walked out.

Dean followed him back out onto the damp walkway. "But that was all good news, right? I mean, we know when, now, and there's a plan, and we're going to see Emalie...."

Oliver leaned on the wooden railing and stared out into the darkness of space in all directions. Light spray from the Acheron cataract tingled on his cheek. "Yeah," he said. Dean was right, but still.... "It doesn't change the fact that we're going to have to go to the Gate. Face Illisius, and do... something. Or the world ends. And it's only days away."

"Yeah, well, there's that," said Dean.

"GENTLEMEN." They found one of the spider-like workers beside them. "IF YOU ARE READY FOR RETURN DELIVERY, PLEASE SAY 'RETURN' NOW."

"Return," said Oliver.

A Hermesian demon soared up out of the darkness and hovered, snatching them both in its claws. With furious wing beats, it lifted alongside the waterfall, up and up.

<101>

They flew back over the rock plains, the deep jungle, to the tree house platform.

"USE YOUR COUNTERSIGN TO RETURN TO YOUR TIME-SPACE LOCATION," instructed the speaker. "THANK YOU FOR USING AEONIAN PARCEL SERVICES, AND HAVE A PLEASANT EXISTENCE."

The creature flew off. Oliver and Dean pressed their wrists, and found themselves back in the restaurant booth once more. This time, no one awaited them.

Outside in the damp evening, Dean asked: "What do you want to do now?"

"I'm just gonna go home," said Oliver. With everything that had just happened, Oliver felt like he didn't want to do anything or be anywhere. It was a mix of anticipation and frustration that left him feeling completely drained. "I'll see you tomorrow night."

Oliver walked home, not wanting to take the bus, but just to walk until his jumbled head felt settled.

*   *   *

By the time Oliver got home it was nearing dawn. Phlox and Sebastian were already in their coffin. Oliver climbed into his and shut the lid. His thoughts had calmed down somewhat since the letter. As much as he felt nervous about what was to come, he had also managed to build some new hope. Emalie was coming back. He would see her again, and they would know what the Triad was and they would stand up to Illisius. He didn't know how

<102>

they'd do these things, but it was at least possible. Finally, he felt like there was some hope again. And soon after that, he fell asleep.

Before long, Oliver found himself back in the hallway in his mind, standing at the door to his demon room.

He entered. The first thing he noticed was that a whole row of the bookshelf was now full, each book with a black spine, silver Skrit etched in them. Oliver looked out the cohesion window, through the eyes of Illisius, and saw a very different scene than the last time.

There were people everywhere, bustling in all directions. It was dawn, golden light streaming through hazy air. Up ahead, the light illuminated a thick cloud of smoke that was billowing from the top of a huge, black, steam engine, the words Central Pacific Railroad in giant letters on its side.

Oliver felt like he was there, navigating this crowd, jostling among their shoulders. He saw that the men were dressed in tweed and wore bowler hats, cowboy hats, and thick mustaches. He—well, Illisius, but it felt like he was doing it—glanced left to see that he was walking with someone, a woman in a fine, lace-trimmed lavender dress. Her face was hidden by a pink parasol held over her shoulder.

In the distance there was water and the masts of large sailing vessels, then steep brown hills on the far side of a wide bay. Oliver guessed from the surroundings and the railroad that this might be San Francisco.

"Tickets!"

<103>

Illisius and his companion stopped before a pinstripe-suited conductor who was checking the tickets of passengers before they boarded the train.

"Now boarding! Central Pacific to Reno and points East. And remember folks, your tickets have to have today's date! No jumping ahead 'cause you want to beat the rush out to those new gold strikes. If you're ticket doesn't say March 14th, then you're not getting on board. Last call!"

Illisius and his travel mate reached the conductor. Oliver saw a smooth pale hand reach out, handing two tickets to the man.

"All right, let's see," said the conductor. "Where's your final destination?"

Illisius spoke, and the conductor nodded. He punched their tickets and waved them on, but Oliver was already sinking away, out of the room, upward, back to his coffin, where he awoke with a panicked jolt, his eyes popping open, his arms flailing. He slammed the lid of his coffin open and sat up.

Nearby, Phlox and Sebastian's coffin popped open as well. Phlox started up, pulling a sleeping mask off her eyes. "Oliver, what is it?"

"Illisius," Oliver croaked.

"You had a demon dream?" asked Sebastian wearily.

"He— he...." Oliver could barely get the words out.

"Honey, just relax. What time period was the dream?"

Oliver nodded. "It... late eighteen hundreds...."

"Oh," Phlox sighed, "That's a relief. That's still a decent ways off—"

<104>

"No, mom!" Oliver suddenly shouted.

"What is it, son?" asked Sebastian.

"It's…." Oliver couldn't believe it, wanted to pretend he hadn't heard the words that his ancient demon had spoken, but he had. "Illisius is on his way to Arcana."

<105>

Chapter 9

THE NEW ARCHITECT

"What?" Dean exclaimed. "Illisius goes to Arcana?"

"He's on his way there on March 14th," said Oliver as they hurried down a warmly lit sewer tunnel. "Emalie said it was the thirteenth in her letter. He'll be there in two days. And they don't know he's coming."

"Do you think he's going there for her?" said Dean.

"Yeah. And probably to stop the Orani from learning about the Triad."

"Dude," mumbled Dean. "That's really not good. What are we going to do?"

"Go there," said Oliver.

They pushed through double doors into the Underground Center. It was a busy Saturday night, the ringed levels bustling with well-dressed vampires. The large waterfall that tumbled through the central space into a deep chasm below was sparkling with holiday lights that hovered in the cascading water.

<106>

Oliver and Dean hurried toward the nearest gap in the levels. Dean was wearing a t-shirt again, the mess of skin on his arms causing offended vampires to literally jump away in disgust. It actually made their travels easier.

"Duck," said Oliver as they passed the food court, and the entrance to *L'organo Sanguinante*. Oliver spied Phlox standing by the door, a clipboard in hand. He'd told his parents all about the dream and they'd been worried, but their response had been predictable: *There's nothing we can do*. And there wasn't, not with Half-Light listening. Phlox had made Oliver promise not to try anything dangerous, but she'd said it like she had known better than to think he'd really keep such a promise. Still, it was best she didn't see him now, if for no other reason than it would make her responsible for his actions. If she remained at work, clueless, then she couldn't be blamed.

They were headed down to the Yomi, which was strictly off-limits under Oliver's probation. As soon as they dropped off the last level of the Underground, his ankle shackle would certainly start sounding.

They reached the first gap. Oliver levitated down as Dean leaped beside him.

"I know you want to do something," Dean was saying behind him, "but isn't Chronius just going to say 'no' again?"

"I don't know," muttered Oliver. "If he does, maybe someone else down there will help us. We have to try."

"Yeah, I get that," said Dean, "but... what if that's exactly what Illisius wants you to do? You know, what if it's a trap?"

<107>

"Whatever." Oliver couldn't keep considering every possibility. All it ever led to was them doing nothing. Two years of it. And that just wasn't an option anymore.

They dropped to the next level.

"Oliver!" Dean called as he landed.

"Just come on, Dean! I'm not arguing about this anym—"

"No, Oliver, wait!"

"Dean—"

"Just LOOK!"

Oliver paused just before dropping to the next level and turned. Dean's back was to the gap. He was pointing behind them. Now Oliver saw it, too: a crowd of vampires, all gazing at a cheery storefront. Bright white light beamed out from its glass walls. Even before he had read the neon sign, Oliver was struck with worry. He knew the location of that storefront; he'd glanced warily at that very spot every time he'd been in the Underground over the last two years. But each time it had just been dark, the glass dusty. Now, it was open for business.

Desiree, thought Oliver—

Only then he saw a bright sign in the window:

UNDER NEW MANAGEMENT

He glanced up at the sign above the store:

Dexires' Drug and Alchemy Emporium

"Dexires?" Dean wondered aloud.

"A new Architect for Earth," Oliver guessed, "to replace Desiree."

Oliver was about to move on—he had to stay focused

<108>

if they were going to get to Emalie in time—when a voice spoke in his head: *Oliver. Please come in. We need to speak.*

It wasn't Desiree, but the voice was similar: smooth, calm, and persuasive.

"He wants us to come in," said Oliver.

"Who?"

Oliver nodded toward the store. "The new guy." He started toward the door. As far as he could figure, the Architects were on his side. Then again, he'd thought Desiree was on his side....

He pushed through the crowd and reached the front. Everyone stood in a shallow ring looking at the store, yet no one entered. Oliver stepped into the space. It felt like breaking a barrier, and he could feel the eyes falling on him, but he kept moving and pushed through the revolving glass door, Dean behind him.

The store looked like it had: an almost blindingly bright white light, orderly aisles of boxes and black bottles, the clean tile on which footsteps made no sound. There was a stuffy silence, a thin string of tinny music drifting through it. Oliver felt a familiar twinge of worry. This place was unsettling, but it maybe seemed somehow less sinister now. The corners and recesses no longer held that dark sense of decay that they had when Desiree was in charge.

Oliver and Dean headed for the back counter. Oliver could already see the Architect standing there, a black-scaled creature with short yellow horns, mug-sized gold coin eyes, ten legs and sixteen arms with eight fingers

<109>

each. All eight hands were resting on the high counter, all one hundred twenty eight fingers tapping their pointed nails. It sounded like a rain of pebbles. As Oliver reached the counter, the Architect smiled, revealing enormous, translucent saber teeth.

"Welcome, Oliver, Dean," said the Architect. "I am Dexires. It's a pleasure to meet you."

"Why'd you call me in here?" Oliver asked brusquely. He was determined not to get into some kind of cryptic conversation.

"Yes, I agree," said Dexires, as if reading his thoughts. His voice was smooth like chocolate. "We should be clear with one another. Unlike my sister, I have no desire to deceive you."

"Good times," said Dean.

Dexires continued, "Not really. Oliver, your cohesion has begun. Time has grown short."

"I noticed," muttered Oliver.

"Yes, which is why you do not have time to waste visiting Chronius or trying to find a way to Arcana."

Oliver bristled. "Yeah, well, sorry. That's where we're headed. Is that all?"

"Not quite," said Dexires, his voice growing more serious. "Listen: Chronius will not grant you the time travel permissions you seek. Not just because he's a ruthless businessman, but also because he knows, like I do, that going to Arcana is not your best plan to undo your prophecy. Going there would, as your friend here already suggested, merely deliver you to Illisius sooner."

<110>

"Well, what am I supposed to do then?" Oliver asked, his frustration mounting. "Hey, I have an idea. You're an Architect. Why don't you and your people just undo the prophecy? You made the universe! Can't you just flip a switch and turn the prophecy off, or something?"

Dexires seemed to smile. His teeth clicked together. The lights in the mirror behind him glowed brightly. "That would be nice, I suppose, but when we built the universe, we did not give ourselves access to its fundamental operation. We can't, as you say, turn off a switch, or rewrite the code, or whatever metaphor you prefer."

"Why not?" asked Dean. "Wouldn't that have made sense?"

"On the contrary," said Dexires. "It would have been cheating. The point of the universe is to see what happens, not to *control* what happens. That's the art of it."

"But you say you can't change things," said Oliver, "and then you set up these shops and give advice and stuff. How is that different?"

"It's completely different. Most obviously because you have the choice whether or not to accept our assistance. We have opinions, of course, preferences as to how we'd like things to go, and part of the thrill of the whole construct is to see what we can influence and what we can't. We are participants in the universe, not operators."

"You make it sound like the universe is a game," said Oliver.

"Not exactly a game, but I'd be lying if I didn't admit that it's something of an experiment. For everything we

<III>

designed so carefully, once we set the universe in motion, it became a creation of its inhabitants and their choices. We participate by making our choices, then you make yours, back to us, and around it goes. Now, can we get down to specifics here?"

"Fine."

"Good. Here is some of my influence which you, as free beings of the universe, can choose to take or leave. Now, I believe you know about the coming Great Radiance and its importance for you."

"Yeah," said Oliver.

"Well, the radiance presents the path of least resistance for bringing you to Nexia in one piece. It's not easy to transport matter multi-world. This alignment is a big reason why your prophecy is unfolding now. You could say that hundreds of years of preparation have all been aimed at next Tuesday at eleven fifteen P.M.," said Dexires, "and twenty three seconds."

"That's not even four days from now," Oliver said quietly.

"Yes, tick tock," said Dexires mildly. "That is why I am here now. It's time for you to prepare."

"But how do I prepare?"

Dexires smiled. "There are two things you need. One is the Triad of Finity."

Oliver felt his entire body tense with frustration. "Wait, so, I've been trying to figure out what the Triad is for two years, and now you're just going to show up and tell me? You couldn't have done that before now?"

<112>

"Oh, no, not me," said Dexires. "I actually don't know what the Triad of Finity is."

"How could you not know?" said Dean. "You made the Universe!"

"As I explained, we set the universe in motion, but it has made its own rules and secrets since we created it. Much like parents, we learn that our children have lives of their own. Again, it's part of the fun, and the surprises are one of the things we Architects derive the most pleasure from. The Triad of Finity is one of those mysteries. Even the Nexia Prophecy is somewhat mystifying to us. Probably the only thing that isn't a mystery is why these things have happened here, on Earth."

"And why's that?" Oliver asked.

"Because this world, Earth, is where life is strongest. Of all the designs in the universe, life is the highest achievement of the Architects. It was as much Desiree's idea as anyone's, actually."

"I thought living beings were looked down on by the higher worlds," said Oliver. "I've been taught that my whole life."

"They may be, but that's just because the dead and the demons don't fully understand what a living being truly is, what it is made of. Its capacity to feel, not just emotions, but stimulus, even time... its extremes of joy and pain.... Those qualities are more intense here than anywhere else in the universe. It's astounding. If something was going to be powerful enough to open the Gate and destroy the universe, it would most certainly be created here on Earth."

<113>

"I was alive once," said Dean sarcastically. "It wasn't that great."

"You have to see it in context," said Dexires. "A vampire or a zombie may seemingly have more powers, like being able to jump high, but a living being has a power in its heart that nonliving beings can never know."

Oliver could believe that. He thought of how Nathan made him feel, or Emalie. But still.... "This doesn't help us," he said. "If you don't know what the Triad is, then what good are you?"

"Now now, let's keep our manners, shall we? I may not know what the Triad is, but I can tell you the other thing you need to do to prepare."

"What's that?"

Dexires reached under the counter.

"Is this the part where you give us some strange bottle or something?" Dean asked.

"Close." Dexires placed an object on the counter. A white moonflower in a glass vial.

"Lythia's group is using those," said Oliver.

"Yes," said Dexires, "and their meeting is tonight at the sewer club called Pele's Lair."

"We know that," said Oliver.

"It is vitally important that you attend that meeting," said Dexires. "Ideally unobserved. To that end...." He reached beneath the counter and produced a little glass jar. He removed the top and a little white creature rolled out, its smooth body about an inch long and slippery.

"What's that?" asked Oliver.

<114>

"Albino Dampening leech," said Dexires. "Place it on the back of your neck. As it feeds on your force energy, it will emit a frequency that blocks the Half-Light tracking device. You'll be invisible to them."

Oliver picked up the little squirming creature between his fingers. He frowned.

"I wouldn't suggest leaving it on for more than a couple hours, otherwise you might start to feel a bit lightheaded. But that should be all the time you need for the meeting."

"But," Oliver began, "why should we go there? Who cares about what Lythia is up to when Emalie—"

"Again," said Dexires, "I am just telling you these things. You will choose what to do. But I am saying that what is happening at Pele's Lair is vitally important to the coming fruition of your prophecy."

Dexires glanced back at the glowing mirror behind him. The lights bobbed around in circular motions. Oliver knew that these lights were the other Architects. The mirrors were how they communicated. "We all urge you to attend," Dexires added.

"But Emalie is—"

"Yes, Emalie," interrupted Dexires. "We have watched the young Orani girl, and I have even met her mother, and one thing I know for certain is that she can take care of herself. Your arrival in Arcana would only complicate things, if you could even get there, which you can't. So please, don't waste your time."

A few of Dexires' fingers rolled the flower toward him. "Trust me. Trust us."

<115>

"I trusted *you* before," Oliver muttered. "And it got my brother slain."

"I know. And for that, all I can offer is my apology." Dexires paused for a moment, then continued. "The flower is an invitation. Take it. And use the leech."

Oliver reached back and placed the leech on his neck. He felt a quick sting as its teeth attached. Then, he slipped the vial into his sweatshirt pocket. "Can you at least tell me what Lythia is up to and save me the trip?"

"I want you to see it for yourself," said Dexires. "Experience is important. Vital actually, when it comes to choice. Things will make sense afterward." Dexires smiled, his many teeth glistening. "The meeting starts soon, Oliver. You should hurry along. And we want you to know that we will be watching, and waiting to help further when we can."

Oliver nodded. "Fine."

"Good," said Dexires. He folded his hands in a clacking of long nails. "It was nice to finally meet you."

"Yeah," said Oliver.

He and Dean headed out. When they emerged, they found the semi-circle crowd staring at them quietly. Oliver recognized a handful of the faces: vampires his parents associated with, parents of kids at school. There were a few high school kids around, too.

Oliver looked at them all looking at him, and it frustrated him so much he wanted to scream.

"I got this," said Dean, and he started enthusiastically forward. "Excuse us!" he said, his dripping elbows causing the gap to widen significantly. They passed through and walked back to the gap between levels.

Oliver gazed downward. It was hard not to keep going, down to the Yomi, to try to get to Arcana....

"Hard to trust the new guy," said Dean, echoing Oliver's thoughts.

"He's probably right about Chronius."

"So you're saying that I was right, too?"

Oliver turned to Dean. "Yeah. Sorry, it's just—"

"I get it," said Dean. "Let's go stalk Lythia. It's always fun to ruin her plans anyway."

"True. And I guess he's right," said Oliver, "about Emalie. She can take care of herself." *I hope*, Oliver thought.

They left the Underground via a side entrance, following a main sewer line beneath Pike Street, toward Capitol Hill.

<117>

Chapter 10

PARTY CRASHERS

A large iron door marked the intersection of the tunnels beneath Pike St. and 11th Ave. The stone floor and walls had begun vibrating around Oliver and Dean a few hundred feet back. The door itself pulsed with bass beats. They reached it just behind a group of teens, who yanked the huge door open by a heavy iron ring. Oliver and Dean followed them into the long hall and were crushed by bodies, sound, and dancing light.

There were no magmalight globes to light the way, no candelabras like in typical vampire tunnels. Here, instead of art on the walls there were shimmering video screens showing a neon blitz of advertising and provocative videos, most in 3-D, with the images jumping out and mixing with the press of bodies. Music shook the walls, everything movement, pressing, every molecule vibrating. Oliver and Dean shuffled along, half-carried by the stream.

Entryways to the different sewer clubs were marked by

<118>

large glowing signs and flanked by tall vampire bouncers in long black coats. Pele's Lair was ahead on the left. The two words in the name were separated by a neon depiction of a tropical island volcano spouting a jet of lava. Most of the sewer clubs were demon-only, meaning you had to have one to get in, but Pele's Lair was all-ages, so the long line outside had a good number of kids in it.

"Head down," said Oliver as they joined the end of the line. He'd spied the seventh Pentath kids from school near the front of the line. He pulled his hoodie over his head.

The line moved slowly. It took almost a half hour for the seventh Pentaths to get in. Oliver and Dean were still a few parties back in the line. Oliver was starting to feel woozy from the leech. He probably needed food, considering this thing was sucking his force energy down.

"Hey, keep your hands off!" A voice screeched. Two bouncers hurried out with a girl thrashing in their arms. "I didn't do anything!" Her eyes were glowing bright, her teeth bared and gnashing. She wore ripped jeans and a t-shirt that was torn at the neck. Her teeth were glossed with neon green glow-polish. It took a moment for Oliver to recognize that it was his former classmate, Carly.

"No brawling in the club," muttered one of the bouncers as they tossed her from the doorway. Carly crashed into the crowd before staggering to her feet.

"She started it!" Carly whined. She lunged back at the door, but the bouncer met her with a stiff arm that sent her airborne, her head cracking against the ceiling before she crumpled to the ground.

<119>

Carly pulled herself up, straightening her shirt. "Whatever," she muttered, and stumbled into others. "Who wants to partyyy?"

Oliver looked down, but then heard Carly say, "Owwliver Nocturrrne?" He looked up just in time to see her careening toward him, her eyes wild. "Hey you!" she called. Oliver tried to act like he didn't know her, but then she crashed into him and threw her arm around his neck.

"Gooood ol', Nocturne," Carly slurred.

"Carly, just, go...." Oliver muttered to her.

"Come on." One of the bouncers was beside them. He grabbed Carly by the arm.

"Cut it out!" she shouted, clawing to hang onto Oliver. Her fingers dug into his neck, right by the area where the leech was.

"Hey!" Oliver reached up, prying at her fingers.

The bouncer kept pulling. "Gaahhh!" Carly shouted. Her hand tore free.

"That's enough from you," the bouncer snarled, and dragged Carly away through the crowd. She thrashed in protest, many in the crowd eyeing her derisively.

Oliver felt around behind his neck.

"You okay?" Dean asked.

Oliver's hand came away with a smear of white guts. "So much for the leech," he said. "We'll have hurry before Half-Light can get here." He looked up. The other bouncer was handling the line on his own. "Come on." Oliver walked up to him. "Hey," he said. "She clawed me bad. Can I head in to wash up?"

<120>

"Go ahead," muttered the bouncer.

They hurried into the dark, humid interior of Pele's Lair, lit in deep red light by open magmalight cascades along the walls. The whole idea was to make it seem like they were inside volcanic caverns. One of the magma cascades fell into a fern-lined pool, freeing huge billows of steam from the roiling water, which clouded the room and made the air hot and moist. Now and then, one of the palm trees in the corners would spontaneously burst into flames. The room hummed with a low soundtrack of island drums and jungle sounds.

Suddenly the music ceased and a piercing shriek grew in volume.

"Whoa, what's that?" Dean asked.

Oliver looked up and saw a screaming, flailing human come hurtling out of the darkness above, grass skirt and flower necklaces whipping in the freefall. Her scream grew deafening just before she plunged into a central pool of magma, causing a small plume of smoke as she was incinerated. The girl hadn't been real, but instead a wax figure with the screaming human projected onto it, though the person used for the terrified projection had no doubt been real. Still, the effect was fairly convincing.

Oliver scanned the club. "See them?"

"Not yet."

They moved quickly along the side of the room, passing deep velvet booths. Oliver wondered how long it would take Half-Light to send someone after him. Ten minutes?

"There," said Dean. He pointed with his chin. The seventh Pentaths were on the far side of the central lava pool, entering a rock passageway. A glowing sign above it read:

Halemaʻumaʻu Theater

Oliver and Dean circled the pool. It was incredibly hot, waves of heat making the world shimmer. Another muscular bouncer wearing gold-framed sunglasses despite the darkness, stood by the doorway.

"Invitation only," he said as they arrived.

Oliver produced the moonflower glass.

The bouncer motioned with his hand.

They entered a rock hallway that wound back and angled downward before ending at an open doorway. As they neared, Oliver saw an old theater, velvet curtains along its antique wooden walls, but he could barely fathom the scene inside.

The theater was packed, its few hundred seats filled, with more attendees standing along the walls. The crowd was mostly vampires; Oliver sensed that about half of them were kids without demons, the other half a mix of ages, mostly young. There were also some zombies, which was unusual enough, but there were even humans here, too.

And on stage, speaking to the entire crowd, was Lythia. Oliver could see her mouth moving, yet couldn't hear her. He reached forward and his hand buzzed against an invisible energy barrier. A low hissing voice spoke: "*Password.*"

<122>

"The Legion?" Oliver tried.

"*Password*," the voice repeated.

Oliver turned to Dean and shrugged. "Any idea?"

"Nothing," said Dean.

They watched through the barrier as Lythia spoke to the crowd. "Emalie would know how to get through this," Oliver said, and cursed to himself. They were almost out of time!

She's not the only girl who can help. Oliver felt a rush of air and Jenette appeared between them.

"Hey, Jenette," said Oliver. He'd heard that hurt tone in her voice, and felt a little wave of guilt. "I didn't think you couldn't help, I just—"

You just didn't think, she said, *about me, anyway.*

"Well—"

It's okay, Oliver. Jenette sighed. *I'm used to it.* She floated up to the barrier and waved her smoky hand in a circle in front of it. The air rippled and she stuck her hand right through. *Someone else didn't think of me either, or of wraiths anyway. I can get through this. Be right back.* She slithered inside.

A moment later there was a soft hiss, and sound from the meeting seemed to suddenly turn on. Jenette curled back to the doorway. *Got it. There was a crystal cell powering the enchantment.* Jenette held out her hands to reveal the crushed powdery remains.

"Nice work," said Oliver.

Jenette slipped around his shoulders. *See how handy I can be?*

<123>

"You guys need a moment alone?" Dean whispered, elbowing Oliver in the shoulder.

"Shut up both of you," Oliver hissed, feeling a rush of frustration. "Come on, quick."

They slipped in along the back wall and listened.

"The Forsaken Legion will not be forgotten!" Lythia called, her fist raised like she was some kind of revolutionary. This made the crowd respond with shouts, growls and hisses of approval. "The important thing," she continued, "is that everyone be ready to act when the time comes. There are only a few more days. We have to be prepared."

Another figure stood up from the front row. A human, and Oliver knew him at once.

"Dude," whispered Dean. "What's he doing here?"

Oliver just shook his head as Braiden Lang, the leader of the Brotherhood of the Fallen addressed the crowd. The Brotherhood was sworn to protect the Gate, and had at one time sworn to slay Oliver. "Our plan for seizing the Transmitter is in place," Braiden called. "Everyone knows their role. They won't be expecting us."

"They've never thought of us before!" someone shouted from the crowd. Others murmured in agreement. Oliver thought the voice sounded familiar, and then he saw that the speaker was Calyssa Welch, Berthold's mother. Berthold was there beside her. His father, too.

Oliver spied other familiar faces. "Um, Dean," he said, "Autumn's here."

<124>

"What?" Dean followed Oliver's pointing to where she stood along the wall. "Uh boy," said Dean. Then, he added, "What is this group?"

"No clue," said Oliver. He couldn't imagine what all these different groups might have in common.

"You'll receive final instructions in the coming days," Lythia told the crowd.

The shouts of approval grew louder, and then someone called out: "And what about the demon?"

"Leave that to me," said Lythia. "And don't worry, when it happens, you'll all get to watch."

"Does she mean Illisius?" Dean whispered. "How is Lythia going to take on—"

Someone's coming! Jenette hissed.

Oliver heard the footsteps, too. Rushing down the hallway. A tall woman burst into the theater, glancing around, confused, likely wondering where the barrier was. Oliver saw the scar on her cheek; she was Braiden's chief lieutenant in the Brotherhood.

She shouted over the crowd. "Half-Light is here!"

The room erupted in confusion and panic.

"Everybody out!" Lythia called. She hurried off the side of the stage. Vampires leapt to the walls and levitated to the ceiling, escaping via sewer pipes and ducts that stuck out here and there. Zombies and humans rushed for the passageways on either side of the stage.

"Which way?" said Dean.

Oliver looked around at the crowds. Any way would take too long—

<125>

Hang on, said Jenette, wrapping her arms around Dean and Oliver's waists. She pulled them backward, out of the world, into the foggy gray of the Shoals, where they were greeted by the sound of waves and the smell of salt.

Hey, guys. Oliver turned to see Nathan floating quickly toward them. *What's going on?* he asked.

That's what we were trying to figure out, Oliver replied, hating that it was his fault that the meeting was ending before they could figure out what it was for.

Through the window, they saw Half-Light arrive, and it wasn't just one agent, it was an entire team. They burst into the room, their long black coats trailing behind them, led by Sebastian's former coworkers, Leah and Yasmin. A black-robed Reader followed them, the demon's single luminous white eye sweeping the area.

"No sign of Nocturne," called Leah, reading a glowing crystal that flashed through the rainbow spectrum in her hand.

"I thought you said we had him?" Yasmin called. She sounded on-edge.

"We did," said Leah. "But he's gone now."

"Do you think he was part of the meeting?" Yasmin wondered aloud.

"Hard to say."

"I don't think so...." Oliver felt a cold chill of recognition even before the next figure walked into the room. Mr. Crevlyn. He pulled off his broad trench coat and folded it over his arm. "But that doesn't mean he wasn't here. Let's take a closer look...."

<126>

He reached up and began calmly digging his clean, fat finger directly into his eye socket. He yanked his eyeball free with a hollow 'pop'—it was, in fact, glass—revealing a cerulean blue, reptile-like demon eye with a yellow slit of pupil. It cast a narrow beam of blinding light around the room.

That's so not good, said Jenette.

What is it? Oliver asked.

Demon grafting. He implanted a demon eye in place of his own. Looks like it's from a Phrenos demon.

So? Asked Dean.

So, said Jenette, *the Phrenos can see through worlds. He's going to be able to—*

"Ahh," said Mr. Crevlyn as the blue beam swung across their hiding place. Its light burst through the foggy window and into the Shoals, falling right on them.

See us! Jenette finished.

"There you are, Oliver," said Mr. Crevlyn, "and… well, how interesting. Very clever." Mr. Crevlyn's free hand was already in his coat. It emerged holding a short throwing knife. Its blade dripped with molten orange sparks.

Oh no…. said Jenette.

What— Oliver began.

"Little nuisance." Mr. Crevlyn's face tightened in concentration. His arm cocked back and he hurled the knife. It spun toward them, leaving a smoke trail as it burned the air. Oliver felt frozen, cringing as the blade sliced through the foggy window of reality with a blinding flash. He smelled the heat coming off its ornately carved blade. He couldn't move—

<127>

But the blade sailed by him.

AHH!

Reality rushed at him. Oliver felt Jenette's arm release, and he and Dean fell back into the world. He landed on the theater floor and spun to see Jenette crumpling to the beach, the blade impaled to the hilt by her heart. Nathan stood behind her, bending over quickly to help her—

Then Oliver was yanked around, Leah hauling him to his feet. "There we are," she said.

"What did you do to her?!" Oliver shouted at Mr. Crevyln. He craned to see behind them but the window into the Shoals winked shut.

Mr. Crevlyn placed his glass eye just above the socket, then smacked it back in with his palm. He blinked a few times and smiled down at Oliver. "I rid you of another dangerous distraction, Mr. Nocturne, nothing more." He glanced at Dean. "Really, you are the chosen vessel. Couldn't you associate with better stock?"

"Shut up!" shouted Oliver.

Mr. Crevlyn turned to Yasmin. "Let everyone know that we've found him and he's safe." He turned back to Oliver. "Very dangerous, you coming here, Oliver, but Half-Light understands your curiosity. We too want to know what this Forsaken Legion is up to." The smile widened. "Did you happen to see who was leading them?"

Oliver set his face in stone. Right then, hard as it was to believe, it was clear to him that if Lythia was now an enemy of Half-Light…. "We didn't see anything," he said. "They were already running off when we arrived."

<128>

Mr. Crevlyn peered at Oliver, the smile faltering. "Really? Well, in all this excitement, it's possible that certain details are slipping your mind. Hmm..." He turned to Leah. "I believe we should bring Mr. Nocturne back to my office, briefly. It's possible that his thoughts have been compromised. Not his fault, of course, but I should check his answers with the Menteur's Heart. For his safety."

Leah nodded. "Okay, let's go."

"No—" Oliver tried to struggle, but Leah held him firm.

"Relax, Oliver." Mr. Crevlyn smiled as he slipped on his coat. "You're safe now."

Yasmin grabbed Dean, but more gingerly, her nose wrinkling.

As they walked back up the hall and into the club, Oliver's thoughts raced. Jenette. Could she survive that blade? How would he find out? Nathan would know. Oliver could summon him... but, wait... Had Mr. Crevlyn seen Nathan? Half-Light would still want to destroy Oliver's soul if they had the chance.... Maybe the blade had been meant for Nathan. In which case, Jenette had saved Oliver and his soul.

They were rounding the large open pool of magma in the room's center. As if on cue, one of the screaming wax humans plunged in, incinerating in a puff of smoke. Oliver could relate. Here he was being pushed toward a fate against his choosing, again.

"Hold on." Mr. Crevlyn had stopped, holding up his hand. Oliver could feel the heat wafting from the magma, pressing against him in waves.

<129>

"What is it?" Leah asked, scanning the room. The club was full of normal movement and chatter, laughter, the clinking of glassware.

Mr. Crevlyn cocked his head. "I'm not sure.... I think—"

There was a tearing sound, like the world's largest length of fabric being ripped in two, then a blinding white light as everything exploded.

<130>

Chapter 11

ARCANA BURNS

Oliver was thrown into the air. He could barely understand what was happening, but he knew his body was in flight, high and far. There was force pressing him from the left, a wall of heat, the biting spray of concrete, hot pricks of magma—An explosion. He could make it out now in his peripheral vision; the wall had blown apart, hurling debris, the force of the blast tossing everyone in its vicinity into the air. Oliver perceived other figures in flight: Mr. Crevlyn, Leah, club attendees, their bodies all righting as they levitated, adult vampires with pinpoint control of themselves in space. Oliver wasn't as skilled; he was still flailing, tumbling, the arc of his flight now turning downward. Toward more heat, the burning sensation on his side increasing....

Oliver twisted and saw the magma pool below. He was falling right toward it. He struggled to find the forces, but they were like ropes swaying in a breeze, glancing off

<131>

his fingertips— Still falling, more heat. The surface of the magma not smooth but cracked like an eggshell, a skin of slightly cooled rock in geometric shapes. He was going to burn—

Until something crushed around his midsection and he was jerked upward. Oliver looked down to see an enormous, three-fingered claw around his waist. Its skin was a charred maroon, its fingernails pearl-white.

Oliver felt the heat receding in beating air. He twisted to see that he was in the clutches of a Hermesian demon from Aeonian Parcel Services.

"*Keeeeaaatchhhhhh!*" The creature screamed.

"That was close!" shouted Dean. Oliver saw that he was in the other claw.

The creature banked hard as they approached the far wall, its wing grazing a magma waterfall but flicking it off as if it were nothing. They turned and swooped back over the scattering, shocked crowd.

"PLEASE DON'T BE ALARMED, MR. NOCTURNE, MR. AUNDERS." Oliver looked up at the copper box on the demon's chest. "WE HAVE ANOTHER MESSAGE FOR YOU, MARKED 'URGENT!' IF YOU CHOOSE TO ACCEPT, PLEASE TOUCH YOUR COUNTERSIGN."

They arced back toward the exploded wall. Oliver saw that they were heading for a gaping black hole. A long, narrow fissure, still smoking.

"QUICKLY," advised the voice.

"Now!" Oliver shouted to Dean.

Oliver touched the leaf tattoo and just as they arced

<132>

into the blackness of the fissure there was a stretching feeling of travel, a loss of senses...

Then they were back in the Acheron Delta, soaring over the foggy jungle once more.

"She still has a sense for timing!" Dean called.

Oliver nodded. His relief at being saved from Mr. Crevlyn was tempered with worry for Jenette, and over what this next message would be, but for the moment, he just enjoyed the cool misty air that was hitting his face instead of magma.

They crossed the delta and hurtled down the cliff face, beside the thundering waterfall, and stopped at the same walkway, the same door. One of the spider-like greeters simply motioned them toward the door. Oliver pressed his tattoo to the handle. Stone bolts lurched. The door creaked inward.

They crossed the cramped room. In the flickering firelight, Oliver could see another letter waiting on the coffin-shaped table. It was the same faded paper, stained at the edges, its postmark from Arcana, and scaled with the same red wax impression of a scarab beetle. Oliver slipped his finger under the seal, unfolded the paper and saw those first words:

Hello Boys,

The world blurred.

Oliver and Dean found themselves within the enchantment of the letter, back in Arcana, only this time it was night. Ahead was the Orani homestead, smoke curling from the chimney of the farmhouse, and also from

<133>

the opening in the roof of the large round structure. The lights were off. A three-quarter moon hung low over the distant mountains, setting for the night. The cool, clear black above was painted with uncountable stars and a feathery vein of Milky Way. It was deathly quiet, no humming power lines or distant cars. The only sounds were the occassional stirrings of animals: an owl hoot, the foraging of a raccoon, the distant howl of a coyote.

Then footsteps. Coming up the path from the house. A figure came into view. Emalie. "Guys," she said. She'd traded her 1800's clothes for jeans, a black sweater, her maroon knit hat and puffy green vest. Her hair in two braids. Bag slung over her shoulder. "Thought you'd like to see how I've been spending my nights." She marched past them, up the road.

Oliver and Dean fell in step behind her.

"Emalie!" Oliver started to shout, wanting to warn her about Illisius, but then remembered that it was useless.

She walked quickly, not speaking, down the hill toward town, but then turned right on a small dirt path, a horse trail through the pines. The path wound back and forth up a gradual incline and emerged at a wide clearing on a hill overlooking town: a cemetery. Emalie passed between wooden crosses and rough-chiseled tombstones, some at cockeyed angles. She stopped in the shadow of a crypt made of marble slabs, the only one of its kind in the place.

"Hello, Jedediah," Emalie said pleasantly to the crypt, giving its side a friendly pat. She turned to Oliver and Dean and her voice shifted to a cowboy drawl. "This here's

<134>

Jedediah Roberts, first prospector to strike gold here in Arcana. News of his strike is pretty much what made this town. The railroad would never have passed through here otherwise. Nobody else has actually found any gold yet, but people keep showing up to pan the rivers and dig in the hills. Jedediah died in a cave-in. People think his sister Marlene orchestrated it, on account of her nefarious new husband Carleton, who made his name in iron sales. The son even briefly hired my mom and Aunt Kathleen to try to read Marlene's mind, to prove she was behind it. That was a whole big thing." Emalie paused and laughed to herself. "Sorry, I could go on and on. Really, I was going to write journals of all this, you know, like, send you guys a whole book about these last few months but... time is short now."

Emalie sat down in the dry grass in front of the tomb. There was a small circle of stones, a fire pit, with a pile of sticks beside it. "Have a seat," Emalie said to them. Oliver and Dean did. Emalie busied herself removing items from her bag.

Below, the town of Arcana lay mostly asleep except for the saloon, from which echoed the tinny tones of an upright piano. An occasional bark, a squeal of laughter, a heavy thud and now and then a lonely silhouette staggering home.

"The saloon's busy all night," said Emalie, shaking her head. "Sometimes I like to project myself down there mentally, and get inside their heads. Every once in awhile I can make somebody throw their drink in someone else's

<135>

face, or start a brawl, or whatever. Basic Orani tricks, but it passes the time."

Emalie scraped a match to life and dropped it in among kindling sticks. A small fire jumped to life. She produced a tiny doll, cloth stuffed with straw, a girl, dressed in white clothes. She placed it in the grass. Beside it she put a tiny silk coated box, ornately designed with flowers.

Then something whistled far off in the night. A train.

"That's Illisius," Emalie said quietly. "I know he's coming for me."

"You do?" Oliver asked, uselessly.

"The dead told me," said Emalie. "That train isn't supposed to arrive until tomorrow. Two P.M., once a week, that's when the train always comes, but Illisius killed everyone on board. It's a corpse train, and it's here for me."

"You have to get out of here!" said Dean.

Emalie continued in a calm, dead serious tone. "This is where I come nights when I can't sleep, which is most of them." She motioned with her hand, indicating the tombstones. "Hanging out here is nice; if anyone's died recently, I can talk to their spirit, or there's a few wraiths who come by. Sometimes Merchynts or other beings will show up to gather supplies—graveyards are like Costco for a demon—and we chat about things. I'm better at controlling my interactions. You remember how I used to get kind of overwhelmed by spirit energy.... Mom and Aunt Kathleen have helped me to control that. It's still intense, but I can usually handle it."

<136>

Emalie paused, swallowing before she said, "But earlier today, all those train passengers dying, that was a lot. It knocked me out right in the middle of milking a cow. They were all screaming, men, women, children, and in every one of their last visions, I could see his face. So I got ready. And now..." she pointed out across town. "They're here."

A light speared through the darkness. The black train chugged slowly into the station, its wheels and gears whining. A few drunk stumblers in the street turned and looked quizzically toward the platform. There was no movement, the train just sitting there, hissing, breathing small clouds of steam. Then, two figures emerged. They moved quickly down the steps of the platform and up Main Street, almost seeming to float.

As they passed into the glow of the kerosene streetlights, Oliver saw the tall gentleman, Illisius, in his suit and hat. The sight made him shudder involuntarily. It had been years since that night in the auditorium, and back then he'd only caught a glimpse. This was the first time he'd actually seen him, and even though Illisius didn't look particularly dangerous, Oliver could feel his power, the way that the forces seemed to be attracted to him like a magnet, gathering around him in a swirl.

His companion was a woman in a pink dress with a wide, ruffled skirt. A parasol umbrella hid her face despite the dark of night. She was as tall as Illisius, and Oliver felt a cold certainty that he knew who she was.

"I left the Orani a wake-up call," said Emalie. Oliver watched her as she watched Illisius stroll down the street.

<137>

It was that serious gaze that she sometimes got, eyes wide, seeming at once fearless and yet so completely aware of the grave danger she faced. It reminded him of right before the darkling ball, just before the Merchynt Sylvix had drained her blood. And though she wasn't in a gown like she had been that night, Oliver thought she looked just as beautiful now, painfully so, especially because he was hundreds of years away from her, and had no idea what was about to happen to her.

A low sound grew from below, the beating of horse hooves. Eight horses galloped fiercely into view, charging up Main Street and pulling up in a line. The Orani women dismounted. Their white robes had been traded for jeans, long leather coats and cowboy hats. They looked like lawmen.

Emalie huffed. "Mom's not with them. She's probably looking for me. Ugh! I told her not to worry."

Illisius and his companion stopped in the middle of the street.

"Go back where you came from, demons!" Oliver heard Selene call toward them.

Illisius didn't speak. He extended his hand. Beside him, the parasol lowered.

"Tsk tsk," said Dead Desiree. "Who's calling who a demon, Orani?"

"Oh no," said Oliver.

Desiree extended her hand, same as Illisius. Lines of bright energy began to stream in from all directions, forces gathering at their palms, then erupting as beams of white fire that hurtled toward the Orani. The fire branched,

<138>

aiming at each woman. The Orani struck defensive poses, creating arcing shields of shimmering light, but the firepower surged like flood water, and they were pushed back and scattered.

Wind whipped down the hills toward the battle, gushing around Emalie and through Oliver and Dean.

"We only require the girl," said Illisius. "She's bound to come to me, anyway, so why make this any harder than it has to be?"

"This is going to be something," said Emalie, but instead of watching she stuck a stick into her fire, stoking the blaze. Then she picked up the small white doll and tossed it in.

"In payment," she muttered to herself.

Oliver watched the doll burn, its clothing and fabric charring to black, its bead eyes melting. He wondered what Emalie was paying for, and what she was paying with. Was this more days of happiness, to be stolen from her later in life?

"Emalie what are you doing?" Dean asked worriedly.

"Emalie," Oliver added, glancing below, to where Illisius and Desiree were advancing. "You need to get out of here."

"I'm sure you guys are thinking that I need to get out of here," said Emalie. Oliver thought, despite her set jaw, that he heard a waver in her voice, and saw her eyes trembling. "Well, that's the plan," she said.

"Emalie!" a voice called from somewhere behind them in the forest.

<139>

Emalie's head whirled. "Crap!" She cursed to herself. "That's Mom. Why doesn't she ever listen to me? I have to hurry." She picked up the silk box.

The wind increased, whistling between the gravestones. The disruption of forces was causing an atmospheric disturbance; large clouds billowed into existence overhead, their bellies reflecting the flashes of the fight. Thunder rumbled. Townspeople began emerging from the saloon and opening windows in other buildings, only to be blown backward.

Emalie opened the small box and reached inside. Her fingers emerged clutching a plum-sized creature: a black, crusty beetle with a fiery, iridescent red back. Its sharp legs flailed. She held it up in front of her face.

Oliver knew what it was, and suddenly, with cold horror, he knew her plan. "Emalie no!" He instinctively swatted at her hand, but of course his slipped right through.

Emalie turned to him and Dean. "You're not going to like this, but just trust me. And Oliver, when the time comes, you need to remember these words: *Now, it's your turn.*"

"What do you mean?" Oliver called. And then he saw her hand moving— "No!"

Emalie shoved the beetle into her mouth. She crunched down on it, wincing, then gulped it down. "Ugh," she muttered, "That was terr—"

Her eyes suddenly rolled back in her head. In the glow of battle light from below, Oliver saw her skin seem to

<140>

crystallize, the blood draining from her cheeks. Her mouth stuck open, her breath dying in her throat, and she fell back to the grass.

"Emalie!" Dean cried.

But the world of the letter was already fading around them.

"No!" Oliver protested again.

And then the fire-filled night in Arcana swirled away, dissolving in a white blur, and Oliver and Dean found themselves back in the stone chamber, breathless.

"Did she just—" Dean began, but didn't finish.

Oliver just stared at him as if to say, *yes*. "That was a Reaper beetle. They're full of lethal toxin. She... probably thought it was the only way to avoid the prophecy...." But even as the words were coming out, it just didn't sound much like Emalie. It was too simple. Then a thought occurred to him, and he felt himself sway on his feet.

"What?" Dean asked.

But Oliver didn't answer. He dropped the letter to the floor, and looked at the long, coffin-sized table before them. He'd already noticed that the padlock on its front was still there, but now he saw that it was unlatched.

He pulled off the lock, hurling it across the room, and hauled open the heavy lid.

Inside was the still body of Emalie.

<141>

Chapter 12

ARRIVALS AND DEPARTURES

"Is she dead?" asked Dean.

Oliver looked at her. Emalie. Right here beneath them. Still dressed in the clothes they'd seen in the letter. If Oliver understood correctly, Emalie was only three months older than when she'd left for Arcana. And she looked the same, really, except....

Her lips were blue, her eyelids a bruised purple. There was a thin film of dust across her face, almost like powder.

"She's been lying here for over two hundred years," said Dean, "hasn't she?"

Oliver nodded. "She must have paid Aeonian Services to take her away that night, right after the letter ended." Oliver felt a burst of relief. "So, Illisius didn't get her, otherwise she wouldn't be here."

Dean stared down at her. "But she's dead."

Oliver considered the bluish tinges, the pale color of her skin. It definitely looked lifeless... He bent over and

<142>

aimed his sensitive vampire ear at her heart. Nothing. "But," he said, "she's not dead, otherwise that blue color would be gone. The blood would've evaporated. And even if this box was airtight, there would still be necrosis, bacteria, mold—"

"You mean she'd look like me," said Dean.

"Worse, probably," said Oliver. "So, it's probably some kind of eternal sleep type enchantment. Her body's in something like Staesys, where everything is slowed down to the point where it's imperceptible."

"You mean she's hibernating?"

"Basically. The question is how to wake her up." Oliver glanced around the edges of the box. Maybe there was a potion, or an incantation to read, some instruction for who to contact... but there was nothing in the box other than Emalie and her bag, which was clutched tight under her crossed arms. He thought about checking her pockets but he didn't want to touch her while she was like this. "There's got to be something." He started looking around the corners of the room.

"That's some fairy tale stuff," said Dean absently. "Sleeping beauty and all that."

Oliver stopped in his tracks. A nervous spike drove into his gut. "Oh no." He returned to the coffin.

"What?" Dean asked.

Oliver gripped the stone edge of the box with both hands. "Fairy tale stuff," he said blankly. He felt like his head had detached from his body, like he was unsticking from gravity.

<143>

"So?"

"So, she said to remember those words: *now it's my turn.*"

"Your turn to what?" Dean asked. "I don't—" his eyes widened. "Oh."

Oliver looked up at him nervously.

Dean burst out laughing. "If that's how she made the enchantment, she might be the most evil of all of us!"

"Great," Oliver said weakly. It made sense. And while it made him tight and uncomfortable like he was in wrong-sized skin made of sandpaper, it was also kind of amazing because it meant that....

Dean sighed loudly. "Hello! End of the world is Tuesday, lover boy. Get on with it."

"Right," said Oliver. He looked at Emalie's pale, blue-tinted face. At her sleeping eyes. At her lips....

And he leaned in and kissed her.

It wasn't warm. Her lips were cold, but still somewhat soft, maybe like kissing a vinyl patio chair, or something else outdoors that was slightly damp and mostly smooth, but yet also smelled just a touch like mildew and death. He pressed his lips against hers, and though he still felt that weightless loss of balance, like his anchor had lifted and he was floating on a sea, he also felt disappointed. This thing he'd been thinking about for two years, that he'd imagined a million ways... it wasn't supposed to go like this. Technically, this was his first kiss, after all, and—

Suddenly a hand clamped on the back of Oliver's neck. His eyes popped open and there were Emalie's wide, dark

<144>

irises, pupils huge, staring at him, her fingers digging into his skin—

"Gah!" Oliver pulled away as Emalie bolted up. Her mouth was open, her eyes bugging, arms flailing in stiff motions like she was made of metal with rusted joints. Her face contorted and she grabbed at her throat. Her mouth opened but there was no sound.

"She can't breathe!" Dean rushed behind her, threw his arms around her waist and pulled in quick thrusts.

Emalie convulsed, her face turning bright red, her eyes watering. Dean pulled again. She made a hacking sound and something shot from her mouth, hitting Oliver in the face with a splat. The crushed shell of the Reaper beetle fell to the floor.

Emalie hauled in a gallon of air, her body heaving, then she gasped and coughed viciously. Her legs began to twitch, her hands rubbing around her neck as if something heavy had just been removed.

"Emalie," said Dean. He patted her back. "Hey, cuz. Welcome back."

Emalie blinked hard then looked up. She turned and saw Dean, then she looked at Oliver. She nodded slowly. "Whoa," she said hoarsely. She gazed around at the stone room. "It worked." She looked back to Oliver. "You figured out what to do."

Then she smiled. Dead for two hundred years, but her devilish nature was alive and well.

Oliver looked away. "Yeah."

"Nice touch," said Dean sarcastically.

<145>

"Ooh," Emalie was trying to swing her legs over the side of the coffin, but winced.

"Here," said Dean. He hoisted her out and placed her on her feet.

Emalie wobbled for a second before gaining her footing. She brushed the centuries of dust off her clothes. "Thanks," she said to Dean, and for just a second her gaze fell on Dean's ruined skin. "It's not going well, is it?"

"No," said Dean. "But it's better now that you're back. And I'll be okay."

"It's good..." Oliver began, but then paused. He wanted her to know how glad he was to see her, how much he'd missed her, but he wanted to say it just right—

Emalie laughed. "Don't hurt yourself," she said. "I'm glad to be back, too." She threw out her arms and wrapped them both in a quick, tight hug. "I missed you both."

Oliver felt like his words were still lost, but Dean said, "We missed you, too."

Emalie pulled away. "Blech." She hacked and made a sick face. "I eat bugs far too often with you guys." She turned and grabbed her shoulder bag from the coffin. "Okay, first things first: I brought souvenirs!"

She rooted in her bag and removed a necklace, which she handed to Dean. "New Hindrian charm for you, to resist Lythia's orders." She searched around more. "And for Oliver, we have..." She pulled out a small glass jar that seemed to be filled with soil. "Here it is. We need to get that ankle thingy off you."

Oliver looked at the jar. "How?"

<146>

"Pull up your jeans and I'll show ya." She winked at him and knelt down. Oliver did as he was told. Emalie unscrewed the top of the jar and dug her fingers inside. "Heeeeere we are." She pulled out a small, black flatworm. She held it by its end as it squirmed. "Okay, don't make any sudden movements...." She knelt down and held the worm directly above the ankle sensor.

"What is it with this sensor and slimy things?" Dean wondered aloud.

Oliver just watched. "You know what you're doing, right?"

"In theory," said Emalie. She pulled a small dagger from her bag and sliced the worm open. Black juice bubbled out, the drops falling, and as soon as they hit the metal, it began to hiss and make a small black cloud. "Don't let it touch you," she warned.

"Right," said Oliver. It already had touched him and the pain was unreal, but he saw that the worm's juices were dissolving the ankle bracelet. A moment later he was able to flick it free. Only a little bit of his flesh was tattooed and smoking from the process.

"Thanks," said Oliver.

"Don't mention it," said Emalie. She reached into her bag again and removed a diamond-shaped mirror with a jade border. "I have this, too. I borrowed it from my mom, in case we need to contact the Architects."

"Nice," said Dean.

"Now," said Emalie, "time to get to work."

Oliver just watched as Emalie rummaged through her

<147>

bag again. Here she was, finally back, and it was business as usual. Oliver didn't know what he'd expected, but he felt a little frustrated by it.

There will be plenty of time to catch up after we save the world, Emalie suddenly said inside his head.

Oliver flinched. Her thought felt like an electric charge through his mind.

Dean rolled his eyes. "Here we go again. You guys are doing your telepathy thing, aren't you?"

"Sorry," Emalie said to Dean. She glanced at Oliver. "It's... okay, right? I mean, I could stay out...."

"No, it's fine," said Oliver, and he thought that it was. Having Emalie's voice in his head, and the knowledge that she was hearing his thoughts: actually it was the least alone he'd felt in a long time.

Good. Oliver found her smiling at him, and smiled back.

Emalie produced a metal square with a convex crystal dome in the middle. Inside, a needle moved over a shimmering map of stars, planets and worlds. "Nexial clock," said Emalie, holding it out. "Kind of like a sundial. We have about two-and-a-half days until the Great Radiance, it looks like."

"Yeah," Oliver agreed. "It's Tuesday night."

"Okay, then we should get moving." Emalie started across the room toward the door.

Oliver and Dean naturally fell into step behind her.

"Where are we going?" Oliver asked.

Emalie didn't answer at first. She opened the door and

<148>

stepped out onto the walkway. "Wow," she said, leaning over and taking in the shimmering waterfall, the space below, the endless doors. "This is amazing."

Oliver stepped to the railing beside her and watched her take it all in, the spirit lights shimmering on her face.

"Be free, little spirits," said Emalie. She turned to Oliver and Dean. "I'm not sure."

"Of what?" Oliver asked.

"Where we're going. But I know who we're looking for."

"We're looking for a who?" asked Dean.

Emalie nodded. "The one who knows what the Triad of Finity is. The only one who ever actually spoke of it first-hand."

"Who's that?" asked Oliver.

"Her name is Theia. She's the oldest Orani, almost three hundred years old, we think. None of the living Orani have ever actually seen her, but we know she's out there. We can feel her presence. We were trying to locate her, but Illisius arrived before we could figure out where she was."

"I don't understand," said Dean. "If this Theia person is Orani, like you, why wouldn't she want you to know where she is?"

"I'm sure she wants us to," said Emalie, "but she can't. She's a prisoner of Half-Light, and has been for a couple hundred years. And nobody knows where they're keeping her. She's not at the Asylum Colony in Morosia. We were able to probe the minds of some of the employees. We

<149>

know that she used to be there, but they moved her to another lab, somewhere hidden and top secret."

"So," said Dean, "We have to find her to figure out what the Triad is."

"She's the only one who knows," said Emalie.

"Well," Oliver began, "but, how did Selene find out that there even was a Triad, if nobody knows what it is?"

"When Selene was in the Asylum Colony, Theia was still there. And so Selene could hear her thoughts, almost like a radio—Orani are connected like that; it's like how I used to see visions of my mom's journeys through time—and so Selene heard Theia going on and on about this Triad, and how it was the key to undoing the prophecy, but she couldn't decipher exactly what it was. Selene says that Theia didn't sound well." Emalie's tone darkened. "She's been experimented on for centuries, at this point."

"How are we going to find her, then?" Dean asked.

Emalie shrugged. "I think our best bet is the Yomi. There's got to be some demon down there who doesn't want the world to end and would help us. Orani knowledge is always valuable."

"Hey," said Dean, "Speaking of: what happened to the rest of the Orani, back in Arcana? Illisius didn't... get them, did he?"

Emalie closed her eyes for a moment, almost like she was searching around in her head. "They're okay," she said. "Once I was gone, they got out of there. Sounds like there were a few injuries but nothing too bad."

<150>

"So where are they now?"

"Safe," said Emalie, "And getting ready to meet us in Nexia."

"And what about Illisius and Desiree?"

"Don't know," said Emalie.

Hearing all of this filled Oliver with excitement and newfound energy. He was ready to get moving, to get back to the action of undoing his prophecy, but the mention of injuries had just reminded him of another wounded friend. He looked seriously at Dean. "Jenette."

"Oh... yeah." Dean nodded solemnly. "We should go see how she's doing."

"What happened to her?" Emalie asked.

"Where to start...." said Dean. "Okay, so, we were headed to the sewer clubs last night..."

As Dean recounted the story, Oliver closed his eyes and spoke slowly. "*Revelethh... lucenthh... persechhh....*"

A dot of light appeared, growing into a disc of pale white, forming arms and legs, a body, and then Nathan was standing before them.

Where have you been? he asked worriedly.

"Lots happening," said Oliver, waving a hand toward Emalie. "Can you take us to Jenette?"

Nathan nodded. *Yeah... but Oliver, it's not good.*

"Okay."

Everybody hang on. Nathan reached for Oliver's hand. Oliver in turn reached back for Emalie's, and she took Dean's. *Ready?*

Oliver felt Nathan tug his arm, and then he felt like

<151>

he was sliding forward. The black of the cliff faded into gray fog, and the roar of the waterfall was replaced by the raspy sound of waves sliding over rocks at the Shoals. Fog hung low, erasing the top of the high sand dune as well as the ocean just beyond the rocky shore.

They walked along the beach. Oliver spied Nathan's little driftwood house. He longed to stop inside and take a look at the sunny street where his human parents lived. How were they doing? How was little Peter? It would be nice to just sit and watch them for awhile, going about their humdrum human lives, having no idea that their world might soon end.

Where are all the wraiths? asked Dean, looking around.

Up here, said Nathan.

Ahead, Oliver saw them—his quick-counting brain estimated over fifty just that he could see—all huddled together. With their mostly human appearance here, they looked like a crowd around an accident, and Oliver's gut twisted with worry.

The crowd parted, letting Nathan and the trio through. Oliver found Jenette lying in the sand, her head on a dirty, blue-and-white striped pillow. Her eyes were closed. She looked so little, lying there. Her frog pajamas were stained black around her sternum, where the blade had hit her.

The four kneeled around her.

Hey Jenette, said Oliver.

Hey.... said Jenette weakly. Her eyelids fluttered open, the gray spaces behind seeming deep and dark. *Where have you*—she spied Emalie—*oh.*

<152>

Hi, said Emalie. *Sorry about what happened.*

We came as soon as we could, said Oliver.

How can we help? Dean asked.

You can't, said Jenette. Her voice was thin, weak. *That blade was advanced force technology. Crevlyn was aiming for Nathan... but you need him, Oliver. And you're both my closest friends.*

Thanks, said Oliver.

So, said Dean, *what? You can't be cured?*

There's got to be an enchantment, said Emalie. *I could—*

No. Jenette reached up and her little hand grazed Oliver's wrist, then settled in his palm. She squeezed. Oliver squeezed back. *My mom slipped into a coma two days ago. She's going, Oliver, and so am I.*

Jenette, don't, said Oliver. *We need—*

Me? Jenette seemed to laugh. *No, you don't, Oliver.* She nodded at Emalie, and the slight pout was detectable in her voice when she said: *You have her.*

That note of jealousy just made Oliver sad; he hated how he'd gotten frustrated by such little things in the past, instead of being kinder. Maybe it was just having Nathan around, but he didn't want to lose Jenette. She was a friend. And she'd suffered so much. Oliver wanted to scream at the Architects, at Half-Light, at the Gate itself. How was this fair?

And Dean and Nathan, Jenette went on. *You have them, too. You'll be fine....* She groaned, a small, hollow sound. *Now listen, remember what I told you, about a*

<153>

wraith? We can be freed if someone agrees to take our grief. I had to choose someone, perform the ritual. You remember how I said that?

Yeah, said Oliver.

To choose someone, you mark them, Jenette continued. *Then, if they are still in your sphere after at least twelve moon cycles, they can choose to accept your grief.*

How do you mark someone? Dean asked.

With a kiss.

Huh, said Oliver. Then he saw Jenette looking at him. And then he remembered.

When Jenette had rescued him from the Brotherhood in the Space Needle years ago.... She'd held him safely in the Shoals until Sebastian and Bane and Half-Light arrived. They had been standing there and just before she sent him back, she'd leaned over and kissed—

You KISSED? Emalie exclaimed, reading his thoughts.

What? Oliver turned. *No! I mean, not exactly. She kissed me, just on the cheek. I didn't—*

Emalie huffed.

Oh relax, Emalie, said Jenette, her attitude sharp despite her weak state. *He's always been yours, but...* Her grip on Oliver's hand tightened. *Oliver, you and Nathan are the only person I've ever known who seemed like a real friend, someone I could trust. I—I knew you'd be strong enough, so I chose you to take my grief, if... if you don't mind. I know it's a burden.*

It might only be until Tuesday, anyway, Dean pointed out.

<154>

Dean... Oliver snapped. He blinked hard. Jenette was dying because she'd saved Nathan. And now she needed his help to be free.... *Okay,* he said. *I'll do it.*

Jenette smiled. *Thanks.* Her other hand reached up and took his. *The wraiths will administer the transfer when I say the last part of the ritual.*

Right now? said Oliver.

Jenette seemed to sniffle. *Right now. This wound isn't going to heal. It hurts so much.... And besides, you guys have a world to save, remember?*

Yeah.

But, Oliver, said Jenette, *remember what I said about my grief. It has power, too. It binds. You can use that power to attach something to you, to keep something close, for forever even, if you want.*

Oliver nodded. *Okay.* He fought the urge to look at Emalie, and tried to shove the thought out of his mind before she could hear it.

If you ever want to use that power, said Jenette, *the incantation is: Contenethh. Don't forget that, okay?* She seemed to glance over his shoulder as she said this—maybe she was guessing what he'd just been thinking about Emalie—but then she gripped his hands with surprising force and pulled him close.

Okay, time to go. Just one more thing....

Sure, said Oliver.

Jenette smiled. Her smoky eyes blinked, as if phantom tears were falling. *Miss me, okay?*

Oliver nodded. And without thinking, he kissed her cheek.

<155>

He thought Emalie might comment, but she was silent.

That was nice, said Jenette. She seemed to take a deep breath. *Release...* she said slowly.

The wraiths held out their hands. Jenette's body began to glow, orange light growing from within, consuming her, the outline of her face, her hands, all becoming light, blinding Oliver's vision.

Then the wraiths screamed at once, an ear-bursting high-pitched wail of sorrow that would have shattered windows were there any nearby.

Jenette's body vanished, and the light rushed up Oliver's hands, up his arms, and sank into him.

As it melted through his clothes, into his skin, it felt like blocks of stone were being lowered onto his chest, onto his arms and legs. A lump formed in his throat, and he felt his head sag. His insides seemed to have grown colder, damp, like the chill of a rain-swept dawn. He could feel the grief settling into his hollow spaces, tucking into his joints, huddling, heavy in the bottoms of his lungs, and he wondered if he would ever be quite as happy again, not that he'd ever been very good at that to begin with.

You'll be okay, said Nathan, rubbing his shoulder.

Oliver wanted to agree, but he could barely lift his head to nod. He gazed at the sand. It was charred black in the place where the little ghost girl had been. She had saved him from peril more times than he could count. *I will miss you*, he thought, and reached down, grabbed a fistful of the blackened sand, and placed it in his pocket.

<156>

Then, he struggled to his feet. The wraiths were drifting away, one by one, to take up their lonely posts and stare out at the starry sea.

Emalie touched his shoulder gently. *We should go,* she said.

Yeah, Oliver agreed. He turned to Nathan. *I'm not sure when we'll see you again.*

Summon me to Nexia, said Nathan. *You're going to need all the help you can get.*

But— Oliver began.

But nothing, said Nathan. *If the world's going to end anyway, I want to be there, to fight with you. There's no point trying to keep me safe anymore.*

You can fight? Dean asked.

I might have a few tricks up my sleeve, said Nathan. *Remember, I'm connected to Oliver, so I can channel his fighting skills, I think. If not, I'll fight Illisius with skipped rocks.*

Okay, said Oliver. He turned to Dean and Emalie.

Is the Yomi still the plan? Dean asked.

Better than going home, said Oliver. He could imagine Mr. Crevlyn waiting there for him, ready to interrogate him.... *Wait a minute.*

What's up? asked Dean.

Oliver looked at Emalie. A thought had occurred to him. *You said Half-Light has Theia.* He couldn't believe it hadn't occurred to him before. *I think I know someone who can tell us where they're holding her.*

Who? Emalie asked.

<157>

Mr. Crevlyn. He was in charge of the Asylum Colony. And he ran their demosapien tests, like on Selene and others.

At this, Emalie's jaw tightened. *Then we should ask him.*

Yeah, but, how are we going to take him? said Dean. *He's got, like, demon parts and stuff.*

Oliver had to agree. *And even if we hit him with an enchantment and get the information from him, he'll bring all of Half-Light down on us.*

Ooh, what if we do the sleep thing, with the memory rite? Dean asked. *You know, where we go into people's dreams, like we did to try to figure out who my master was?*

Oliver shook his head. *Crevlyn's too strong. I think he'd be ready for that.*

Yeah, Emalie agreed. *I don't think we can sneak into his head. Humans are one thing....*

Hold on, said Oliver. He'd been thinking about sneaking around, about doing something without someone knowing. *What if....* It was crazy, but maybe perfect. Dean had mentioned their dream hopping, which made him think of.... *I think I know who can help us.*

<158>

Chapter 13

THE FORSAKEN LEGION

It was a foggy near-dawn, the world a smoky blue when the Hermesian demon popped into reality and lowered Oliver, Emalie and Dean to their destination. Oliver had to steady himself, which was mostly because of where they were now standing, but maybe also slightly because he and Emalie had just flown across the Delta sharing a claw, squeezed shoulder-to-shoulder, hip-to-hip, with Emalie being all warm and alive-smelling again.

They had devised a plan for their secret entry, and for how best to abduct their prey and escape before security forces descended on them, but as they climbed along the side of the structure, they found that all of their planning had been wasted effort.

There were no security guards on the wooden dock beside the large, white yacht.

And their target was already outside, almost like she was waiting for them.

<159>

But she wasn't. She was kneeling out at the end of the bow, dressed in a black leather jacket and a long dark purple skirt, her hair hanging around her face as she gazed down into the fog-cloaked water. Oliver heard her mumbling to herself. Then she reached her hands between the metal railing and flicked something outward. White rose petals scattered. They fluttered toward the water, each bursting into a small flame as it descended. They hit the water's surface with a hiss, leaving tiny black swirls of ash.

Emalie was about to release the binding enchantment, but Oliver threw an arm in front of her. He knew this ritual—it was a memorial—and guessed who it was for. And so he waited another few seconds, as the girl knelt in silence, before speaking.

"Lythia—"

"*TachESSS!*" Lythia shot into the air like a pouncing leopard, spinning to face them, a long, thin sword shimmering into existence in her hand.

But Oliver was ready. He'd already formed his two rattan fighting sticks and as Lythia arced toward them he thrust forward, slamming her in the shoulder. The impact sent her careening off course and crashing to the deck. The entire yacht rocked, throwing off everyone's balance.

"*Bind!*" Emalie called, and scattered a handful of iridescent crystal powder over Lythia. The crystals created a spider web of energy lines, forming a thin net that wrapped Lythia tight. Her sword clattered to the deck and Oliver grabbed it.

She writhed against it. "Let me go, you—"

Then she looked up, and seemed to notice Emalie for the first time. Oliver glanced over and saw that Emalie's eyes were glowing: white hot pupils and red irises.

"So, the bloodbag is back," said Lythia, but she also stopped struggling. "Minion, throw the demon child overboard."

Dean stood still, chuckling. "Sorry, master," he said sarcastically. He reached to his neck and showed Lythia the new Hindrian charm that Emalie had provided him with.

Lythia shrugged her eyebrows. "Whatever. You were useless anyway." She glared at Oliver. "Knew you were coming. Sensed you in Pele's Lair before. I may not have my demon, but I'm still powerful."

"I know," said Oliver, though he thought that Lythia didn't look very powerful right then, or just a minute ago when she was performing that memorial ritual. This made him think to say, "Sorry about your brother."

Lythia glared at him. "Who cares if you are."

Oliver wondered what to say, and a silent moment passed between them. Lythia's brother, Alexy, had been prepared to receive the Anointment in Oliver's place. Only the force treatments had made him sick. Last year, he'd finally succumbed to his condition. Lythia had been out of school for a couple weeks. In spite of their past, Oliver had always had an urge to say something to her about it. Now was as good a time as any.

"I know what it's like," said Oliver. "Losing a brother. I know it sucks."

<161>

"Yeah?" Lythia snarled. She got up onto her knees, her eyes flaring lavender. "You know what it's like to have your father lose his career, to be stuck living on a boat 'cause you can't afford anywhere else? To be shut out of Half-Light's big plan and to watch as all the other lucky boys and girls get their free pass to the next universe? AND to lose your brother? What do you know, Nocturne? No matter how bad it's been for you, you're still the chosen boy. You're still going to get to exist beyond the Gate."

Oliver was struck by this. "What are you talking about? What do you mean free passes?"

Lythia chuckled. "You are still an idiot. Didn't it ever occur to you what all those kids in our class, the ones who got their demons early, had in common?"

Oliver hadn't thought about that. He'd been too busy worrying about getting his own demon, and about Emalie. "What?" he asked, hating how clueless he sounded.

"Use your prophecy-boy brain," Lythia muttered.

"Watch it," said Emalie.

"Make me, bloodbag."

"Maybe I will—"

"Hold on," Oliver snapped. He thought about the kids who'd gotten their demons abnormally fast: Carly, Kym, Suzyn and Jesper. What did they all have in common....

Then it he saw it. He couldn't believe he hadn't realized it before. "All their parents work for Half-Light," said Oliver. "And Theo, Maggots, Berthold, and you, now... your parents don't."

"Congratulations," said Lythia. "Half-Light and that

<162>

Dr. Vincent, they figured out a treatment to summon their kids' demons early, whether they were really ready or not."

"Okay," said Oliver. He thought about Carly, out of control in the sewer clubs. She definitely hadn't seemed ready. "But so what?"

"So…" Lythia rolled her eyes, "what does that tell you, Nocturne, about your big destiny, the one that comes true on Tuesday?"

Oliver thought it over… and then he understood. "When the Gate opens, vampires with demons will be free, but, if you don't have a demon…."

"You'd be destroyed like the rest of us," Emalie finished quietly. "You'll be no better than a human."

"Or a zombie," Dean added.

"Poof," said Lythia. "That's why Half-Light has kept the prophecy and the plan such a secret all these years. All us demonless vampire kids who aren't part of their inner circle, we'll be just like all this junk." She waved her hand, seemingly at all of reality around them. "Forsaken."

And now Oliver understood that, too. "Your Forsaken Legion. You, the Brotherhood, zombies, other vampires… you're—"

"An army," said Lythia proudly. "An army of the left-behind."

"An army?" asked Emalie. "But, to fight who, Half-Light?"

"Good girl," said Lythia. She struggled to her feet. "So, are you going to release me or what?"

"Why would we do that?" asked Dean.

<163>

Lythia rolled her eyes. "Sometimes I just can't be-lieve you dimwits are the big heroes. So we can work together. Duh! You obviously have some plan to try to stop the end of the world. That's why you're here, isn't it? And we have ours, so let's just get on with it. Tick tock, you know?"

"You just attacked me with a sword," Oliver pointed out.

Lythia smiled. "Yeah, but that was just for fun. Now, come on. Everybody's waiting."

"Everybody?" asked Emalie.

"The rest of the Legion, or, the high command anyway. We've been hacking into Half-Light's monitoring systems for weeks—know every sorry thing you've done, Nocturne, by watching your ankle sensor, until you disappeared last night, anyway. Still, we figured it would only be a matter of time before you showed up here."

I don't know about this, Emalie thought worriedly in Oliver's mind. *Let's just grab Lythia and run.*

Oliver thought about it. He looked back at Lythia, glanced out at the water, the ash swirls in memory of her lost brother ... *I think we need all the help we can get,* he thought back.

Fine. Emalie sounded annoyed. *Just keep your guard up.*

"Okay," said Oliver.

Emalie waved her hand, and the netting fell away from Lythia.

Lythia's hand shot out. Her sword leapt back into her palm—

<164>

"Hey!" Emalie shouted.

"Relax!" Lythia gripped the sword with both hands. "Just putting it away." She whispered to herself and the sword dissipated into smoke. "This way." She brushed past them, around the side of the ship.

"You're sure about this?" Dean asked quietly.

"As sure as I am about anything these days," said Oliver. He shrugged and followed her.

They reached the back deck. Lythia opened the cabin door and they entered, crossing a living room. They dropped down a steep set of stairs to a narrow, dark-wood hallway lit with tiny magmalight globes. Lythia headed aft, opening a metal bulkhead door. They entered a dimly lit metal room, cluttered with the engine and plumbing. The machinery hummed quietly.

In the far corner of the room, behind a tree of thick pipes, a hatch was bolted into the floor. Lythia began to twist open the iron wheel on top.

"Um, a hatch in the floor of the boat.... Wouldn't that lead into the water?" Dean asked.

"Wow, minion," Lythia muttered, "your grasp of up-and-down is really improving! Smart little zombie."

She popped open the hatch. A ladder led down through a cylindrical metal tunnel. She turned and smiled at them. "Secrets," she said, and dropped down the hatch without using the ladder.

Oliver, Emalie and Dean stood around the edge.

"Are we really about to follow Lythia into a dark place?" Dean asked.

<165>

"Good times," said Oliver flatly, and leapt in.

He dropped further than he thought he would, emerging from the tight tunnel and landing hard on a concrete floor. He moved out of the way as Dean tumbled down.

Coming, said Emalie. She blinked into sight beside them, having used her old force bending trick to levitate down.

Lythia was already stalking off up ahead. The three followed. They were in a tall, round concrete tunnel. The sides were cracked; white salt streaks bordered dark patches that were draped with that slippery seaweed that one might find on tide pool rocks. Here and there, colonies of mussels lined the cracks. Shallow puddles dotted the floor.

"Looks like an old sewer outfall tunnel," said Oliver. "Must not be on the vampire map though, otherwise it would be warmer, and have some art and stuff."

They followed Lythia for five minutes, until the old tunnel ended at a surprisingly new looking steel wall. Lythia spun the wheel on a rectangular hatch door. It swung open with a hiss. Beyond was a small square room. The walls on either side of them were made of sleek steel, but the far wall was curved and old, made of brown, scarred metal. This little room was attached to it with thick rubber padding.

"Is that a submarine?" Dean asked, looking at the markings on the welded metal panels. "A U-Boat? The writing looks like German."

<166>

"You can get them refurbished for cheap in Naraka," said Lythia, yanking open a hatch on the submarine wall with a rusty squeal. She stepped inside, let the trio in, then slammed the door shut behind them. The clang echoed in the darkness.

They walked down a cramped corridor, pipes and metal framing pressing in on either side of them.

"It's nowhere near as nice as the sub we took to the South Pole, when we were tracking The Artifact," said Lythia. "That was a Russian nuclear sub, totally sweet. This works though, at least well enough to bring it here and ditch it in the mud undetected."

"It's pretty cool, as hideouts go," said Dean.

"Why thank you, minion."

They twisted and turned through the tights halls, and arrived in a somewhat more spacious control room.

"Well, here they are." Oliver knew Malcolm LeRoux's voice, and saw him leaning against a bank of controls. Braiden Lang stood nearby. There was his scar-faced second in command. Beside her was Talia LeRoux, Lythia's mother, her hair teal blue and swirled atop her head. Oliver didn't recognize the others: a mix of humans and vampires, about ten in all, manning computer displays. For a World War II sub, it looked like the electronics had been given a major upgrade.

Oliver felt Emalie and Dean press against his shoulders. Here they were. Oliver maybe hadn't considered seriously enough that this could be a trap. No one spoke, so Oliver just started talking. "We came to get Lythia."

<167>

"What for?" Malcolm asked.

"Does it matter?" asked Emalie coldly.

"If you're going to put my daughter in danger," said Talia, "then, yes."

"Tell us what you're doing, first," Emalie countered.

Malcolm traded a look with Braiden. He smiled. "Fine. I assume you know about the coming Great Radiance."

Oliver nodded.

"Well," Malcolm continued, "when Half-Light confirms that you two have been summoned to open the Gate, they will begin transporting their members to Nexia, so they can bear witness to the big event. And besides, Earth won't exactly be the safest place to be once reality starts to disintegrate. Matter can be particularly... pointy, when it's being destroyed.

"Half-Light has a portal device in their headquarters downtown called a Force Axial Transmitter, for transporting everyone. Our plan is to seize control of the Transmitter and go to Nexia."

"And then what?" Oliver asked.

Braiden spoke up, his eyes fixed on the floor. "And then we fight. Try to take out the demon."

"Illisius is powerful," said Oliver, remembering his display in Arcana.

"So he is," said Malcolm.

"And," Oliver added, "Desiree is with him."

This caused a murmur to pass around the room.

"Then we'll fight her as well," said Malcom.

"Whatever it takes to save our children," Talia added.

<168>

"Now," said Malcolm, "what exactly is *your* plan?"

Oliver hesitated, but it seemed the only way forward was to reveal what they were up to. "We're going to find out where Half-Light is keeping Theia, the oldest Orani. She knows what the Triad of Finity is."

"The what?" Malcolm asked.

"Exactly," said Dean.

"It's some kind of safeguard," said Oliver, "that we can use to resist Illisius and keep from opening the Gate. So, if we can find it before we're summoned, we might have a chance."

Malcolm nodded. "It sounds like about as big a long shot as our plan, but I guess two long shots will improve the odds. How can we help?"

Oliver looked at Lythia. "We need to know where you got that orb that you used to freeze time, the night you killed Dean," said Oliver.

Lythia peered at him. "An Orb of Synchrus?"

"Whatever it's called," said Oliver. "We need one, and we need to know how to use it."

"What for?" Lythia asked.

"So that we can interrogate Mr. Crevlyn. We think he knows where Theia is being held."

Lythia's eyes brightened. "And then we could create a false memory so he won't remember afterward," she finished. "Which will give us time to make our getaway."

"Something like that," said Oliver.

Lythia smiled. "I have to say, Nocturne, that's actually pretty smart."

<169>

"We've been tracking Mr. Crevlyn's activities," said Malcolm. "He's currently waiting at your house, figuring you'll return there."

"That's what we were thinking, too," said Oliver.

"So then let's go," said Lythia. "I know just where to get an orb." She looked from Oliver to Emalie to Dean, then nodded with a smile. "Guess I'm finally part of the team."

Emalie huffed at this. Oliver wondered about Lythia's smile. It had always been one of her least trustworthy features. Then again, they had so much loss in common, and they were after the same thing now....

Also, at this point, they had little choice.

"We'll station ourselves outside your house," said Braiden. "Mr. Crevlyn will no doubt have a security team standing by."

"Okay, then," said Oliver, "Here we go." He and Emalie and Dean headed back through the submarine, their new ally trailing behind them.

<170>

Chapter 14

THE LAST DINNER

Morning was gray, but bright enough that Oliver and Dean took the sewers back to Twilight Lane. Sunday morning: two days before the end. The thought made Oliver's body tense, made everything feel tight, and with the addition of Jenette's grief, his movements felt so heavy that he wondered if he could make it through what was to come.

And yet, as real as their circumstances were, and despite all that he knew about the prophecy and the Gate and his destiny, it still seemed impossible that these stone tunnels that he'd known all his life could actually be destroyed. Or the heavy wooden door he was opening now. Their crypt, coffins, his school, all of it.

He stepped inside and looked back at Dean. Dean shrugged his eyebrows. A new crack had broken open on his temple. A black line of infected fluid ran down his cheek and neck, staining the collar of his t-shirt. He

<171>

rubbed at it now, looked at the stained finger, and sighed. "I don't suppose the Triad of Finity can fix my skin."

"Probably not." Oliver listened; the house was silent. He knew what awaited him upstairs, but pretending he didn't was essential to the plan. "Hello?" he called.

"Up here, Oliver," Phlox answered. He could hear the tension in her voice.

"Here we go," Oliver said quietly to Dean. The two walked up the stone spiral staircase, crossed through the kitchen, and entered the living room.

"Well, well, here he is." Mr. Crevlyn sat on the chair opposite the couch, grinning at Oliver. "Home safe at last." His codex knelt on a pillow beside him. Incense burned in the stone bowl in front of him. Mr. Crevlyn already had the Menteur's Heart out. It lay on its black velvet on the coffee table, glowing pink.

"I must say it is a great relief to see you, Oliver," said Mr. Crevlyn, his smile so wide it seemed as if he had extra teeth. "I've already spoken with your parents, to fill them in on what happened with you last night. They were quite surprised to hear of your appearance at the sewer clubs, and also that you made a trip to the Underground."

Oliver glanced at Phlox and Sebastian. They weren't looking at him.

"But they were most surprised to hear of your exit from Pele's Lair," Mr. Crevlyn continued, "and full of worry as to where you'd gone. I have to say I share their concern. So, let's try to straighten everything out here, shall we? First off, I believe I observed you being whisked away by

<172>

an Aeonian courier demon. I assume it brought you out to their post office boxes at the Acheron Cataract."

"Yeah," said Oliver.

"And so, why were you brought there?"

"To get a package."

"What kind of package?"

Just then, there was the clicking of the door opening downstairs.

Oliver looked at Mr. Crevlyn, and returned his smile. "See for yourself."

Two sets of footsteps clopped up the stairs to the kitchen.

"What's going on?" Mr. Crevlyn's smile lessened, his teeth disappearing like a light dimming.

"Oliver...." Phlox said quietly. He looked over and saw the worry in her eyes. He hated having to do all this without informing them, but there'd been no other way. Oliver tried to say as much with a shrug of his brow.

Voices echoed from the kitchen.

Emalie's: "No way, you put that in his drink?"

And Lythia's: "Sure did. It was so gross. His mouth foamed for like two days, but he got what he deserved."

"Man, you're twisted," Emalie said. Oliver couldn't be sure, but it sounded friendly. Were Emalie and Lythia bantering?

They sauntered into the living room hip to hip. They were about the same height, and if it hadn't been for the living and dead colors of their skin, respectively, someone might have mistaken them for sisters.

<173>

Oliver could barely believe it. Lythia had asked for Emalie's help procuring the orb of Synchrus in the Yomi, as the Merchynt was notoriously hard to bargain with, and Lythia no longer had a demon. Emalie thought it was a good idea, mainly so she could keep an eye on Lythia. The plan had been for Oliver and Dean to go ahead and put Mr. Crevlyn at ease. But Lythia and Emalie becoming pals had not been part of the plan.

"Hello, everyone," said Lythia.

Oliver saw Mr. Crevlyn staring at Emalie. His smile was still missing, but his eyes had widened. He looked, almost... hungry.

Emalie gazed right back at him. "'Sup."

"Well," Mr. Crevlyn hummed, "the Anointed Orani, the Muse, Eos, Emalie. You've returned. All is coming full circle."

"You have no idea," said Lythia. She pulled her hand from behind her back, revealing a staff with the blue crystal orb at the top, same as the one Bane had brought to the school gym, so long ago.

Mr. Crevlyn's eyes darkened. "Well now...."

Lythia slammed the staff against the floor, and blue iridescent light exploded from the orb, washing over the room in a flood. As before, everything turned topaz, the walls, the furniture, even the air getting still, dust particles hovering in mid-drift, only this time, Oliver wasn't frozen. Nor were Dean, Emalie, Lythia, Phlox and Sebastian. Only Mr. Crevlyn and the codex had been stilled, their skin frosty.

<174>

Lythia leaned the staff against the wall and walked over to Mr. Crevlyn. She put a hand on his head and quietly muttered unintelligible demon words. His face suddenly stirred like he was awake, but his skin was still blue, and his eyes remained closed.

Meanwhile, Emalie picked up the glowing Menteur's Heart from the table. She whispered to it in demon tongues and it glowed brighter; she'd changed its purpose from detecting lies to preventing them outright.

Emalie held the crystal up to him. "*Obey,*" she hissed, her eyes glowing red. She blew on the stone, and a wisp of pink-colored smoke curled off of it and over Mr. Crevlyn's face.

Mr. Crevlyn spoke hoarsely. "What have you done?"

"Turned the tables," said Lythia. She looked at Emalie. "Go ahead."

Emalie sat down on the coffee table in front of Crevlyn, leaning toward him like a hard-boiled interrogator. "Tell us where to find the oldest Orani."

"You... I...." Mr. Crevlyn seemed to be trying to resist, to say something else, but he couldn't fight the Menteur's Heart. "We are keeping her in the research facility beneath the island of Amchitka."

"Of course," said Sebastian. "That's in the Aleutian Islands, practically in Russia. It's a top secret facility, easily hidden because there's still some fallout there from nuclear testing."

"How do we get in?" Emalie asked. "Are there passwords?"

<175>

"No passwords, only guardian demons. The only way you'll get in is to fight."

"And do you know what the Triad of Finity is?" asked Emalie.

"The Triad…." Mr. Crevlyn's face contorted, again as if he was trying to resist answering. "That is a riddle we have long been trying to solve. We've performed centuries of tests, but the demosapien woman only speaks in gibberish, unconnected thoughts.

"She repeats triplets of words," Crevlyn continued. "Earth, Eve, Dawn. Light, Dark, Choice. We are unsure as to their exact meaning. And with all the tests, it's been decades since she could respond coherently. At this point, the demosapien has no rational thoughts left, near as we can tell."

"That doesn't sound good," said Dean.

"No," Oliver agreed, "but we still—"

"Wait," said Emalie. She peered at Mr. Crevlyn, the look on her face deadly. Her voice lowered with her next question: "What did you mean, 'demosapien'?"

"That is the classification of an Orani," said Mr. Crevlyn. "Or, rather, Orani are a subspecies of the demosapien lines."

"Explain," Emalie growled.

"Demosapiens are humans in which the demon essence is more acutely expressed. All living creatures have a bit of demon inside them; it is a necessary building block for life."

"That's what Dexires was talking about," Dean said to Oliver.

<176>

Oliver nodded.

"In nearly all living beings," said Mr. Crevlyn, "the demon essence exists in balance with the soul, yet in the case of the Orani, the demon is stronger, more… active."

"You're saying I'm part demon?" asked Emalie thinly.

"My dear," said Mr. Crevlyn, "all living beings are. It's just that your demon self is more awake, and you actually feel it, and express it. It's where you get your powers. It's how you feel the forces of the larger universe."

Emalie looked away, her fists clenching.

Mr. Crevlyn seemed to sense this, even though his eyes were still closed. "It's not a bad thing," he continued, his grin inching wider, as if talking about all this pleased him. "In fact, we have found, in other Orani test subjects, that if the demon element is isolated and removed, the subject dies, just the same as if her soul was removed.

"It is quite remarkable," Mr. Crevlyn went on, "how demon and soul coexist within the living vessel. How they need each other. There cannot be good without evil. And the balance of their struggle is Life. That is the Architect's model. They have this whole notion that *feeling* is some great advancement of the universe. Needless to say, it's not part of our plan for the next one."

Oliver was trying to wrap his brain around all this. It seemed important somehow, though he couldn't quite grasp why.

But Emalie was still focused on the Orani. Her voice became a hiss. "How many of my sisters have you killed in these tests?"

<177>

More of Mr. Crevlyn's glossy teeth appeared. "Well, you're a hard breed to catch. Let me think…. I have presided over the removal operations on… about twenty three, dating back to the 1600's, though many of those were during the Salem witch trials, which were a brilliant piece of revisionist history to hide our experiments. Salem was the only time we ever found the Orani Circle of Six and their families in the same place. Silly girls, thinking they'd be safe in the New World. That was where we found and captured Theia—"

"Whoa!" Dean shouted.

Oliver had been half-listening, still lost in his thoughts, but he tore his gaze from the floor and had just enough time to notice that Emalie's hands were over her head, and in them, an enormous Persian Shamshir sword was materializing. Her eyes flared red and she sliced downward.

"Emalie!" Oliver began.

"*Recompenssss!*" She hissed. Oliver knew the Skrit word for 'retribution'—

The sword cleanly beheaded Mr. Crevlyn. The last thing Oliver saw of him was his smug smile tumbling sideways, then disintegrating to ash, along with the rest of his body. Dust pattered on the stone floor.

A moment of utter silence passed over the group. The only sounds were Emalie's short, fast breaths. Oliver watched her eyes change from violent red back to brown, watched her pupils cool from white hot embers to coal black. She handed the blade to Lythia, their eyes meeting.

"Nice work," said Lythia.

<178>

Oliver reached out and touched Emalie's arm. *Had to*, she thought to him.

"No more killing for him," said Oliver.

Emalie nodded in agreement. "Just in case we do save the world, he won't be in it."

"Well then...." Phlox stood up. "I'll get the vacuum."

Dean surveyed the ash on the couch and floor. "This is probably going to make things more complicated."

Sebastian walked over to the table. He picked up the Menteur's Heart, placed it beneath the spotless heel of his shoe, and crushed it into powder. He turned to Lythia. "Can you wake the codex?"

"Sure." Lythia spoke quietly beside his hooded head. The codex hauled in a rattling breath.

Sebastian knelt before him. "What is your wish, ancient one?" he asked.

"*Cindrethhh...*" the codex whispered in his ancient, sandpaper voice, the Skrit to return to ash, or dust.

"Then it shall be," said Sebastian. He gripped the chains that held the codex and tore them apart. As the chains snapped, breaking the spell of eternal existence that was given in exchange for servitude, the Codex crumbled to ash.

Phlox returned with the vacuum. She efficiently plugged it in, fired it up and swept over the stone tile floors, everyone watching silently, their thoughts lost in the hum.

"Oliver." Phlox indicated the coffee table and the chair, having him move each. She changed nozzles and

<179>

cleaned the crevices around the chair cushions. Satisfied, she turned off the machine. "Now then, Lythia, how long will this frozen time sphere remain active?"

"I made it for an hour," Lythia replied. "I figured it would take us awhile to plant the false memory enchantments in Mr. Crevlyn's head, so he'd never know what happened, but... well, we've got most of that time back now, I guess."

Phlox nodded. "Good. If I work fast, that's just enough time for dinner."

"But, mom," said Oliver. "We have to go! We only have two days to get to Amchitka, and once Half-Light finds out about Mr. Crevlyn, not to mention that we're gone, they're going to throw everything they have after us and—"

"All the more reason to have a full stomachs," she said, quickly wrapping the vacuum cord back up.

Was she crazy? "Mom, no! We need to get—"

"Oliver!" Phlox's eyes flared turquoise, and her voice grew quiet and lethal. "We are going to sit down and have dinner, and that is the end of it."

"You heard your mother," echoed Sebastian.

Oliver wanted to scream. How could she be this irrational? Except... maybe he understood. Because maybe Phlox was thinking, like he was, that this might be it: their last time in this house, their last time together.

"Fine," he muttered.

"Good." Phlox's eyes cooled. "Now, kids, Oliver can show you where to find the dishes to set the table.

<180>

Sebastian, take drink orders. I just happen to have a double chocolate angel food cake in the freezer, and I believe there's some Scotch bonnet peppers in the pantry; I can whip up a quick sauce."

Everyone started to move, and no one questioned the idea, or really spoke. Ten minutes later, the Nocturnes, Dean, Emalie and Lythia were seated at the dining room table. Sebastian turned down the magmalights to a nice orange glow, and turned the radio to KBYT, which was playing a late movement of the Melancholia.

Oliver and Lythia drank panda blood, one of Oliver's all time favorites, and the rarest variety they had in the fridge. Dean thought it was too tangy, and opted for basic pig. Phlox and Sebastian had their customary goblets of human blood. Emalie had a Coke.

"Oof," Emalie winced at her first bite of the cake dipped in sauce. "That is the spiciest thing I've ever had." Tears leaked from the corners of her eyes.

"You should try these," said Dean as he cracked open a frozen gila monster head and began sucking out the insides.

Emalie scowled at him. "Yeah, I'm good, thanks. Still tasting that Reaper beetle's guts."

"Well," said Phlox, dabbing her magenta lips with a bone white napkin, "I have to say, that was an impressive plan you executed down there, kids, despite the—" she glanced at Emalie with an ever-so-slight expression of disapproval—"ending. Either way, I was really proud of you all."

<181>

"Thanks, mom," said Oliver.

"Delicious food, honey," said Sebastian.

"Thank you, dear."

"Yeah, Mrs. Nocturne," said Lythia, "after we save the world, my mom totally needs to take some lessons from you."

"That's sweet, Lythia. It would be nice to see more of the LeRoux's. All those years at Half-Light and I feel like we barely got to know them. This prophecy was always a source of tension between us."

A silence passed over the group.

"Hey, did you guys catch if the Seahawks won?" asked Dean. "They were playing a Saturday night game."

Everyone just looked at him.

Dean smiled. "Right, I'm the only zombie here. Never mind. I'm just thinking, if it was their last game ever, I hope they went out on a high note."

Silence again.

Forks scraped on plates. Cups raised and clicked back onto the table.

"I put on coffee," said Sebastian, standing. "Anyone want some?"

Everyone nodded.

"Sebastian, use the Ming china," Phlox called after him.

"Do I—" he began, but then caught Phlox's eye and nodded. "Okay."

He returned with a steel carafe and a tray of exquisite china coffee cups, ornately decorated with curving, intertwined dragons. He poured cups and passed them

<182>

around, followed by a bowl of sugar cubes and a habañero pepper grinder.

"I'll pass," said Emalie, handing the shaker to Dean.

Oliver went to sip his coffee and noticed that his hand was shaking. His whole body felt tight, like he was tied with invisible rope. He looked around at his family and friends—well, and Lythia—and felt another rushing round of that tightness like when he was entering the house. All this: could it really be about to end?

A final silence passed between them.

Oliver met Phlox's eyes. Her gaze was deadly serious. "Okay," she said. "Now that we've eaten... what's next?"

"We'll need an initial diversion," said Sebastian. "Something to confuse Half-Light. Then, we need transport out of town."

"Charions?" suggested Oliver.

Sebastian shook his head. "We'd never get down to the station and onto a train in time."

"Airplane?" asked Dean.

"We'd need advance planning, space in cargo to avoid the sun... and again, there won't be time."

"How about a submarine?" asked Lythia.

Phlox gazed at her. "You have a submarine?"

"Not personally, but the Legion does."

Phlox turned to Sebastian. "Didn't you drive subs briefly in World War II?"

"Not exactly," said Sebastian, "I manned sonar, but I could—"

A hissing sound cut him off.

<183>

"Ooh," said Lythia, gazing around. The blue tint was fading from the walls. "I think the enchantment is finishing early. I had to estimate."

The blue winked out. Immediately, there was vicious banging from below, at the sewer door. It grew fierce, and there were sharp splintering noises as the heavy wood began to crack.

"So much for our head start," said Sebastian. "Crevlyn must have had a security enchantment that would alert them if he was harmed."

"Well then," Phlox said again. She looked at the table, not at the guests, but at the plates and cups, it seemed, and sighed. Oliver thought he saw the shine of a tear in the corner of her eye, though that was impossible....

Sebastian reached over and grasped her hand.

Phlox nodded, as if checking off a moment in her mind.

A vicious cracking sounded from below. The door was giving way.

"Honey," said Phlox quietly, still gazing into the table. "Get the battle axes from the hall closet."

Sebastian slipped out of his chair.

Phlox looked up. "Everyone else, head upstairs." She reached up and began tying back her hair. "Oliver, the reflector umbrellas are in the wall recess by the surface door." She stood. "We'll meet you outside."

"Mom, we—"

"I know you want to help," said Phlox, standing. Sebastian leaned in from the kitchen and tossed her a burly, medieval horseman's axe. Phlox caught it in one

<184>

hand. "But your father and I have been sitting on the sidelines for too long. Let us get our hands dirty." She almost seemed to smile, then she turned and raced toward the sound of the collapsing door.

Oliver looked around the table. "Let's go."

They rushed out of the dining room, across the kitchen, up the stairs—and for just a moment, Oliver looked back at the kitchen, the dinner dishes piled by the sink. He had the weirdest thought: wanting to stop and clean them, make everything look just right, the way it had every night of his childhood, the way it should look every night forever—

"Come on." Emalie tugged his arm.

The sounds of clanging metal and hissing screeches at their backs, Oliver followed Emalie, Dean and Lythia up the stairs to the surface door. He pushed aside what appeared to be just another loose board and grabbed four specially coated black umbrellas for repelling the daylight. He handed them to Lythia and pressed the red button to open the door. He kicked the old refrigerator out of the way, sending it flying across the room and smashing into the standing mirror. Just before impact, Oliver saw the round impression of the spot that Emalie had once cleared in the decades old grime. The mirror exploded.

They vaulted the false hole and hurried out the front door, down the spider-web-laced walkway, the overgrown blackberry vines clutching at their legs.

Out in the street, Oliver popped open an umbrella. The sky was hazy with misting clouds, but bright enough to make his eyes hurt.

<185>

"What happened?" Braiden Lang emerged from behind nearby cars, along with two of his Brotherhood soldiers.

"Company," said Lythia. She nodded at Emalie. "'Loose cannon' here dusted Mr. Crevlyn." She actually sounded impressed as she said it.

Oliver watched the still house. He could hear the sounds of a fight beneath the surface. Loud thumps, the smashing of furniture, walls... then silence.

Footsteps.

Shadows by the door.... Phlox and Sebastian emerged, their faces dusted with ash, axes over their shoulders. Sebastian had his long coat on, and now paused to hold out Phlox's. He took her axe and she slipped her arms through and took back her weapon. They walked down the path and joined Oliver and his friends in the street. Oliver handed them an umbrella.

The rain began to intensify, pattering on the street.

"How'd it go?" Oliver asked.

"That was refreshing," said Phlox. She wiped ash from her eyelids and turned back to gaze at the warped, dilapidated house, its windows boarded, its sides consumed by blackberry and overgrown rhododendrons. Oliver stepped beside her. She slipped her arm around him. "It was good," said Phlox quietly. "A good house. A good time, all in all."

Oliver nodded, but couldn't get any words out.

Something screeched from above. Oliver looked up to see a crow circling above them.

"That's probably a sentry," said Braiden.

<186>

"We should move," said Sebastian. "Where is this submarine?"

"It's at my dad's yacht," said Lythia.

"Okay, then let's—"

But Oliver cut him off. "No," he said, because if Half-Light had already come after them at the house…. They'd never make it across town and onto a submarine, never mind across the ocean and on from there. Half-Light had too many resources. There was only one way to do this. The tight feeling had become overwhelming. "Dad, mom, you— you can't come."

"Oliver," said Phlox, "what are you—"

"If you come with us, you'll be left behind when Illisius summons us. You need to go with the Legion to Nexia."

"But what about you?" Phlox asked.

Oliver hadn't gotten very far with what to do next, but now it occurred to him. "Dexires," he said. He turned to Emalie. She was already digging into her bag for the Architects' mirror. "The Architects can send us to Amchitka," said Oliver. "They're the only ones with the power to transport us quickly. You guys can hide out with the Legion, plan the attack on Half-Light, and the three of us—"

"Two," said Dean. Oliver turned to find him shrugging. "Think it through, man," he said, "I'm not getting summoned to the Gate. If I want to fight, I have to go with the Legion, too." He didn't look happy about it. "Stay with you and I'll just get left behind."

"He's right," said Emalie. "We can stay in touch

<187>

through our tattoos," she said, touching her wrist, "Like we did for the Darkling Ball."

Oliver looked at Dean. He didn't like it, but knew he was right. "Okay."

"Don't worry," said Lythia, "I'll take good care of my minion."

Dean kicked at the pavement. "This will give me time, too, to go by my house. Let my parents know that they won't need the axes under their beds anymore...." He looked up, almost like he'd been caught thinking something he shouldn't. "Well, at least for a few nights."

"What are you talking about?" Emalie asked.

"Nothing," Oliver said to Emalie, but he nodded at Dean, trying to say that he understood, and to say, somehow, that he was sorry, sorry it had come to this, that Dean was in this position to begin with, sorry about everything... all the way back to the beginning.

"Don't sweat it," said Dean, as if he knew what Oliver was thinking. "If I wasn't like this," he moved his hands to indicate his zombie self, "I'd just be waking up right now like it was any other Sunday. So... get going. It's really going to be a bummer if you don't save the world."

"Right," said Oliver.

"See you soon, cuz." Emalie moved toward Dean, arms out.

"Ahh," said Dean, looking at his oozing arms, "watch out for my—"

"I don't care." Emalie hugged him tight.

"Oliver." He found his parents beside him. "Be careful,"

<188>

said Phlox. "Be in touch through Dean. Find out what the Triad is and... we—" Phlox grimaced. "We're sorry. This prophecy, we...."

"It's okay," Oliver whispered, and threw his arms around them both at once, burying his head between them. He smelled Sebastian's after-shave, the lavender hair gloss Phlox used.... His parents, not by blood, but the ones who knew him. They may have made him a vampire with a terrible destiny, but they'd also raised him, protected him in the best way they knew how.

"We love you," said Sebastian quietly.

Oliver pulled away, biting his lip hard, and nodded in response. Then, fighting the heaviness inside with what felt like all the effort he had left, he turned away.

Emalie held up the Architect's mirror and gazed into the deep blur of bobbing lights within its diamond border.

"Here they come!" Braiden was pointing skyward. A flock of crows and owls were swooping over the rooftops.

Screeching sounds behind them— Three black luxury cars with tinted windows careened around the corner, speeding toward them, water spraying from their tires.

"Get out of here!" Oliver shouted at the rest of them. "I'm the one they want!"

Phlox, Sebastian, Dean, Lythia, Braiden and his team ran into the yards across the street.

"Dexires!" Emalie called into the mirror.

A single sphere of light bobbed closer and came into sharp focus. *Of course*, Dexires said in their minds.

The cars were skidding to a halt. The birds diving,

<189>

dissolving into smoke and forming vampires.

Brilliant white light burst forth from the mirror, and Oliver and Emalie disappeared from Twilight Lane.

* * *

The light faded and Oliver and Emalie found themselves in Dexires's shop, standing at the base of the high counter. He loomed over them, leaning forward on his many hands. His fingers were still. It was quiet, warm. The faint music wafted with the scent of ammonia.

"Welcome back," said Dexires.

"Thanks," said Oliver. "So, do you know where we need to go?"

"Yes, I heard. And are you feeling prepared for the journey?" Dexires asked, and Oliver thought he sounded different somehow, hoarse or something. And it smelled different in here, too; the ammonia was stronger, almost nostril-burning.

"Yeah," said Oliver. "We're ready. The sooner the better—"

"Tut tut, Oliver," said Dexires, only that sounded even less like him, in fact— "Let's not rush through the pleasantries, shall we? After all..."

Dexires seemed to lean farther forward, too far—

He tumbled over the front of the counter. Oliver and Emalie leapt backward as the mass of arms and legs crumpled to the floor, lifeless.

"Oh no," Emalie whispered, looking up.

<190>

Oliver followed her gaze. The red hair. The white coat. The lavender eyes....

"It's been so long," said Dead Desiree smoothly. She looked around her shop with an expression of dissatisfaction. "This place needed a good cleaning." She looked down at them. "But no matter. Now, you're here. And we have so much catching up to do."

She thrust out her hand, and Oliver was blinded with golden light.

<191>

Chapter 15

UPON ANCIENT PLAINS

Oliver's eyes blinked open. He wasn't sure how long he'd been asleep or unconscious, but it seemed like it had been awhile. Distantly, he could feel his arms and legs aching, his head throbbing, his eyes burning like he'd been staring at a bright magmalight for too long. But those sensations were still up on the surface, and he was somewhere inside his head still....

The golden glow that Desiree had created slowly dissipated, scattering like a swarm of luminous fireflies, and Oliver perceived a dark room: the one in his mind. He saw the bookshelves. There were many more leather volumes now. Entire rows were filled in. He saw the wide window. It had changed again.

The view of Nexia was still gone, only now the window was flashing with one quick moment of action after another in a blurring stream. Oliver saw flashes of hundreds of moments: battles, explosions, earthquakes,

<192>

eruptions, people running and screaming, floods.

"Hello, Oliver."

Sitting in the desk chair, the short flashes of imagery covering him in an ever-shifting mask of color, was Illisius. "Amazing, isn't it? My whole history on fast forward, dumping into your brain." Oliver looked to either side and saw books popping into existence on the shelves, filling row after row.

"This will probably give you a headache," said Illisius, "but we have to work fast. Time is short." He turned and folded his hands on the antique desk. A blue china cup of steaming tea sat before him. "It's nice to see you." Illisius smiled. Oliver noticed his white sharp teeth, his clean face and orderly black hair. His eyes gleamed like old bronze weaponry. His smooth fingers were interlocked on the desk.

When Oliver didn't respond, Illisius continued. "It's almost time." He sighed deeply, then swiveled in his chair and gazed out the window. Images of crumbling buildings flickered on his cheek. "You're almost to Nexia, and when you arrive, we'll join and do the great work of our kind."

"I don't want to," said Oliver. He knew it sounded pathetic.

Illisius nodded. "You've been so confused. Pulled in so many directions. It was an impossible job, really. Your human roots, a lingering soul, the Orani girl, all these things pressing the desperate yearnings of Finity onto you like greasy fingerprints. But fear not: after we open the Gate, you'll get over it."

<193>

"I don't want to get over it," said Oliver, thinking of Emalie, Dean, his parents. "I don't want to lose them."

"Ahh," Illisius waved his hand, "Give it a few millennia. You'll see how uninformed those thoughts are. It's so small-minded. The living always think they're the most important thing in the universe. As if there haven't been billions before them, and billions to come after them. As if there weren't trillions of other living beings in parallel worlds right now." He waved his hand at the flashing imagery. "This is just one anthill, if you know what I mean. You widen your gaze enough, and you see how silly all those human emotions are, how silly it is to think that lives *mean* something. But when you're trapped on Earth, you can't see it. You're governed by all these things that you *feel*." Illisius said the word as if it was toxic. "It's not your fault."

Oliver had nothing to say. He thought about that idea: of feeling. Dexires had said it was important, but Illisius made it sound so pathetic. Oliver thought of the night on the bluff when Nathan had given him the ability to feel his sadness over Bane, to cry over it. He thought about the other times: feeling hope for the future, feeling what he felt for Emalie, frustration with his destiny, and how all those feelings were so out of step with the other vampires. And yet...

Maybe it was yet another mark of how screwed up he was, but those were all times he remembered so vividly, and, maybe the times when he felt... alive? *But you're not alive*, he told himself. Well, they were at least the times

<194>

when he felt good, in a way. Something like content. Would he really want to give those up?

"Just think," said Illisius, "You'll be the last true vampire to be created. I'll be the last prisoner. And then the Gate will be opened by a vampire: the very kind of creature that the Architects created to keep their universe safe."

"How exactly am I going to open the Gate?" Oliver asked. No one had ever actually told him that part, and Illisius seemed to be in a chatty mood. Maybe Oliver could figure out what was about to happen, not that he had any hope of stopping it at this point.

"Actually, that's the easiest part," said Illisius. "You're the vampire of the prophecy, and prophecies are simply universal laws that have been revealed, like the code that runs the program. All you have to do is command the Gate to open, and it will. Think of the Gate as needing a password. Well, you're the password. It's as simple as that."

"But I don't want to tell the Gate to open," said Oliver, again hating how useless it sounded.

"Not yet," said Illisius with a smile. He chuckled. "I'll see you soon." He turned back to the flickering blurring window. Oliver saw images of roadside bombs exploding in desert sands. Almost up to the present....

*   *   *

Oliver came to in more darkness. Felt the pains in his

<195>

legs and arms more acutely. And Illisius was right; he had a throbbing headache.

The world around him was shuddering back and forth. He felt vibrating in his feet and teeth. He was sitting on something metal. There was clanging around him, a weird sound like tearing, and he felt nauseous....

Oliver bent forward and wretched. A stream of blood and chocolate splattered against a metal floor. There went dinner. He looked around, his vision swimming. Some kind of metal-walled cell. Judging by the size of the bolts, the walls were thick, possibly lead. A small oil lamp was affixed to the wall, a white flame flickering in a glass globe, beside the impression of a door. There was no handle.

The world vibrated again with a loud hum, and Oliver felt it down into his bones, almost like his entire body was about to disintegrate atom-by-atom....

A hand slipped into his. Suddenly the feeling abated. Oliver looked over to see Emalie beside him. She was sitting on the same bench, slumped against the wall. She looked at him with half-open eyes and smiled weakly. "I'm the one who got Anointed, remember? I have the, what was it called?"

Oliver leaned back, half against the wall and half against her shoulder, grateful for relief. "Transdimensional energy," said Oliver. "The Anointment was supposed to make this trip possible, or something."

Emalie's eyes slipped closed. "Who can even remember, anymore," she mumbled. "I don't feel all that great, but I'm keeping my dinner down. Does my hand help?"

<196>

Oliver had an immediate reply, held it back, thought to say something else, then decided, what the heck, they were on their way to end the world, the least he could do was say what was on his mind. If there was one thing he'd learned from Emalie, from Dean and Nathan, from *life*, it was to say what he felt. "Your hand always helps."

"Mmm." Emalie's smile grew. "You're sweet." She stretched her legs and grimaced. "Everything hurts, though. How did we get in here?"

Oliver looked around the cell. "Desiree. Big flash of light."

"Where do you think *here* is?"

The whole room shivered again. There was a distant crashing sound like thunder. "No idea," said Oliver. "But I think we're a long way from Earth now. I saw Illisius in my mind. He said we were close to Nexia. So, I guess it's Tuesday."

"I've been trying to contact Dean," said Emalie, "or the Orani. Anybody. All I can hear is static."

She pulled his hand and took it in both of hers. "I'm glad I'm here with you. Glad you don't have to do this alone."

"I missed you," said Oliver.

"I missed you, too." She leaned over and kissed him, their lips touching for a second...

Two... warm, radiating energy through Oliver's entire body, making bright sparks in his mind.

Three... then she leaned back against the wall.

Oliver just stared into space. He wanted to be happy

<197>

about that, the kissing, how amazing it felt, how natural it was, like it was meant to be, and yet, how could he be? That kissing was a part of a world that, in a matter of hours, they were doomed to end.

"We didn't get the Triad," said Emalie.

Oliver just shook his head. "Nope." What hope did they have now? He thought back to his prophecy, hearing it in Selene's wispy voice, years ago.

He recited it softly: "*There will come a young demonless vampire who has garnered a power never before known among them, and who will at maturity be able to open the Nexia Gate. The moment of choice will require a vessel so strong it can overcome the most powerful forces of the Architects. This triumph will free the* vampyr, *and establish a new order.*"

Oliver glanced at Emalie. She was supposedly the power that the prophecy referred to, and yet Illisius hadn't mentioned what Emalie's role in opening the Gate was. Maybe they were supposed to command it open together. And, Illisius hadn't said anything about a moment of choice. What choice?

"Weird," Oliver said aloud.

"Hmm?" said Emalie.

"My prophecy says there will be a moment of choice."

"Like, whether or not to open the Gate?" Emalie thought aloud.

"Maybe," said Oliver. "Crevlyn said something about a choice, too." What had it been…. "He said the Oldest Orani was always saying triplets of words. Um… Earth,

<198>

Eve, Dawn. And Light, Dark, Choice."

"Those are triads," said Emalie. "I mean, threes right? Maybe they're code. Code for the Triad of Finity."

"Yeah but, what do they mean?"

The room vibrated again. There was a wicked splintering sound from somewhere above them, and the room lurched. Oliver was tossed into Emalie. He felt his bones shuddering, felt like he might throw up again. She squeezed his hand tighter. It helped. Oliver looked around, wishing he could see out.

"Well," said Emalie. "Eve is like Dark. Then, Light and Dawn are similar. Earth and Choice don't match up at all, though."

There was a shrieking sound, and their room seemed to bounce roughly off something. Oliver felt their velocity slow. He wondered if they were arriving.

"Wait," he said. "The Orani: you said they called you Eos."

"Yeah, for dawn," said Emalie. She sat up. "Oh, and... you live by night. What if you're dark? And I'm dawn. And a third person could be Earth...."

Oliver met her wide eyes. "What if Earth means, like, ground? Dean crawled up from the earth. And he didn't have a choice about his existence, because of having a Master...." Oliver couldn't believe what he was thinking. "Could it be... us?"

Emalie nodded. "Maybe we're the Triad." She smiled at the idea. "But what does that mean? What would we do?"

<199>

"Selene said to gather the Triad, and that we'd be able to resist opening the Gate."

"Well, Dean is on his way. Oliver, this could be it! It's US! We—"

"Shhh!" Oliver threw a hand over Emalie's mouth, feeling the warm wet of her lips and breath but he had to ignore that because someone was coming.

The door squealed open. Desiree stepped in. She was wearing high boots, khaki pants and a long, black leather coat. It was singed in places. Her blood red hair was tied back, and she had thick aviator goggles pulled up onto her forehead. Oliver noticed a black mark, like ash, on her cheek.

"Hello, children." She motioned out the doorway. "It's been quite a journey. We left a little before the Great Radiance actually began so things have been a little rough, but all is aligned now and it's safe to come out. We're arriving at Nexia. I thought you'd like to see." She started out.

Oliver held Emalie's hand tight and they both stood. They ducked out of the tiny room and found themselves in a low-ceilinged hallway. The violent sounds from outside had ceased, and Oliver could feel a gentle swaying. Emalie took hold of the back of his sweatshirt with her free hand, as she had on their first adventure into the Underground. Oliver had to fight back a shudder. It hurt to remember that beginning, now that they were at the end. Hurt to consider that this could be the last time she grabbed his sweatshirt, and yet, he reminded himself, if they were right

<200>

about the Triad, then maybe, just maybe, they could pull this off.

They were treading on grated metal. Below was curving superstructure that reminded Oliver of the hull of a boat. To either side were windowless doors similar to the one they'd just exited. Other holding chambers, Oliver guessed. Lined cells for transporting beings between worlds.

Desiree reached a short, steep staircase and popped up out of sight. Oliver stopped, feeling Emalie behind him. "This is it," he said hoarsely.

"Go," said Emalie, and he could suddenly hear that old confidence in her voice. "We're the Triad. We got this."

Oliver nodded. He released her hand, grabbed the handrails and climbed up.

They emerged on an open platform, the flat top of a vessel shaped somewhat like a boat, with a pointed bow and a square back. The deck was level from front to back and made of long black planks. Part of the low railing around its perimeter was on fire near the back. There were slashes in the wood too, like burn marks.

Huge steel cables were tied to thick iron rings and led up to a large gray zeppelin. Oliver glanced back and saw small, skeletal black creatures, similar to those that assisted at Aeonian Courier Services, all wearing goggles. They stood by a bank of controls and a large brass wheel, piloting the airship. Two others were working to extinguish the fire.

"Up here," called Desiree. She stood ahead, at the point of the bow.

<201>

They stepped beside her. Despite their plight, Oliver still couldn't resist a tremor of wonder at the view before them.

Nexia. Oliver remembered it from his dream in the school gym; there were the brilliantly clear planets, galaxies and nebulae in the sky; the globular, luminous blobs that were individual worlds, spinning across the pure black, all so close you felt like you could jump and touch them; below, the blood red, canyon-riddled plains stretching in all directions; the curving amethyst and jade spires, mostly toppled and broken, dotting the uneven land; and in the distance, a hazy glow on the horizon.

The Gate. Though it was miles away, Oliver could still make out a sense of vertical metal, a massive structure, and even from this distance the light made him squint.

"It's really lovely," said Desiree, "Don't you think? Took us ages to construct."

"I don't understand why you don't just open it yourself," said Emalie, squinting at the light. "I mean, if you built it, don't you like, have a key or something?"

Desiree looked down at her and smiled. "You're welcome, by the way."

"For what?" Emalie snapped.

"For starters, safe transport across thirty five worlds," said Desiree. "That's not an easy journey. Then, Emalie, I've given you an enchantment to survive here in a world with no air. After all, who would want to miss your sassy comments?

"But," she continued, "to answer your question: no

<202>

individual Architect has the power to open the Gate. It's the lynch pin, the final brick in the wall, if you will, of the universe. And building the universe took us a long time. So, we Architects built the Gate so that we could only open it if we were in unanimous agreement. Needless to say, we're not, and probably never will be."

"You can't open it, but a vampire and a girl from Earth can," said Emalie.

"Yes, that's how it turned out," said Desiree. She smiled at this. "These are exactly the kind of surprises that make universe-building so fun. I can't wait to do the next one."

The airship was nearing the ground. Oliver saw a road beneath them, saw a stagecoach parked on the crushed obsidian. The creatures on deck scuttled about, throwing ropes over the sides of the ship. One lowered a rope ladder.

"This way," said Desiree. Oliver and Emalie followed her to the ladder. "Now I'll go first." She swung her leg over the railing. "And please, don't waste anyone's time trying to get away. I don't want to have to damage you before we get there." She smiled and started down.

Emalie rolled her eyes. "Never liked her," she muttered.

Oliver tried to smile at this, but it didn't quite form. Too many nerves now, jangling inside him, a symphony of vibrations all off-key with one another.

They climbed down the creaking ladder. Their sneakers crunched on the curved shards of black glass. Each footstep slid before catching. Desiree stepped into the stagecoach. Oliver looked at the large zombie horses, their mud-colored hair and red eyes, their thick hooves

<203>

crushing the glass to powder as they stamped impatiently. The coach was painted dark red with black and gold trim. Its windows were hung with black velvet curtains. There was no driver sitting atop it.

Oliver and Emalie climbed inside. One of the creatures closed the door. The horses immediately started to tug forward, increasing speed, their feet crashing on the glass. Despite the rough road, the coach's ride was smooth.

Desiree sat across from them. "Comfortable, isn't it?"

Oliver and Emalie didn't reply.

"Do you like my new skin?" Desiree pushed back her sleeve and ran her long black-painted index fingernail up and down her wrist. "I had my Merchynt tailor add in the veins this time, or, should I say, harvest the veins, too. I think it gives me a more realistic look."

"That's disgusting," said Emalie.

"Tuh," clucked Desiree. "What do you think your leather belt is made out of, deary: smiles and hugs?"

"Why are you even in that disguise?" Oliver asked.

"For old time's sake," said Desiree. "Once we open the Gate, this human form will be obsolete."

Oliver pulled back the curtain and watched the landscape blur by. They were moving incredibly fast. Each outcropping of rock or fallen crystal building had a long dark shadow trailing behind it like a cape. As they traveled, the shadows grew shorter, the golden glow on the face of everything getting brighter. The light of the Gate....

Oliver. See me clearly.

The voice spoke in his mind and Oliver remembered it

from his first dream of this place. It was the voice of the Gate itself. He'd heard that phrase somewhere else too… but he couldn't remember where. What did it mean?

What did what mean? Emalie thought to him.

"What are you two scheming about over there?" Desiree asked, peering at them.

"Nothing," said Oliver quickly, remembering that Desiree could read their thoughts too. And yet it seemed like neither she nor Emalie had heard the Gate just now. Only him.

Outside, the light was growing. Oliver had to squint just to make out the landscape. They were passing a crumbling amphitheater, made entirely of jade.

All at once, the coach stopped.

"And here we are." Desiree smiled. Oliver saw her skin ripple strangely, the real mouth of giant teeth, the huge coin eyes and horns moving on their own beneath her costume. "Showtime, kids."

She ushered them out the door. Oliver dropped down onto the road and had to shield his eyes against the all-encompassing brightness. He looked up to see the Gate towering over them, still a few hundred yards away but hundreds of feet tall, a massive golden door on thick hinges, but attached to nothing. Standing free on the plain, casting its light in all directions.

"Whoa," Emalie breathed. She was squinting up at it. Peering more closely, Oliver could see that its entire surface was engraved with designs: Stars, demons, creatures, all in intricate detail, intertwining: a mural of every aspect of the entire universe.

<205>

"This way," said Desiree. She rounded the stagecoach. Oliver and Emalie followed. A stone path led across the red plain, weaving between the crystal ruins. Oliver could see that ahead, it led to a jutting table of rock that rose up at an angle out of the plains, like the bow of a half-sunken ship. It reached toward the gate, ending at a flat mesa top with steep cliffs on all sides. Oliver could see a wide jade staircase twisting up the side. There was a structure up there, too, some kind of temple ringed by columns.

Oliver felt a deep shudder. That was the spot where it would end. His legs tingled. He felt like he was swimming in his head. Emalie kept a tight hold of his hand.

As they neared the staircase, Oliver could now see that there were others here: vampires lining the stairs, all the way up to the top: Half-Light, all dressed nicely, like for a formal event. Of course, this *was* a formal event, and one that Half-Light had been planning for a long time. They must have begun arriving once they knew that Oliver and Emalie had been caught.

"Why are you even working with them?" Emalie asked Desiree.

"Convenience," said Desiree off-handedly. "We realized after that whole episode at the Darkling Ball that we both want the same thing. Why hold grudges?"

They started up the stairs, and Oliver saw that, like the Gate, each jade step was carved with every creature imaginable, slithering and sliding together.

They passed the vampires, who watched them in silence. Oliver recognized many of the faces. Some nodded

<206>

approvingly at him: the chosen one, finally making good. And each group that they passed fell into step behind him, a procession of the undead.

A flash of light caught his eye. Halfway up the staircase, there was a flat ledge carved out of the side of the incline. On it was a silver, diamond-shaped pedestal. The flash was another group of vampires arriving, from the Transmitter at Half-Light. They stepped down and moved toward the stairs just as Oliver and Emalie passed.

What do you think is happening back there? Oliver thought to Emalie.

Don't know, said Emalie. *I keep trying to contact Dean, but I can't find him.*

They kept climbing, past hundreds of vampires. Oliver felt warm Gate light on his cheek.

The stairs ended at the round temple, its columns and half-crumbled roof built entirely of amethyst crystal. Instead of entering, they turned left and walked out along the narrow, flat plateau, heading directly into the brilliant Gate light. They passed the last vampires, who stood in a semi-circle facing the Gate.

Ahead, his form a narrow eclipse of the light, was a tall thin man in a long, hooded robe. He stood just before the pointed end of the plateau, in the center of a disc of solid gold, twenty feet in diameter. It was etched with a detailed map of orbiting worlds and planets. Skrit markings ringed its edge. It gleamed, nearly blinding in the Gate light.

The man turned and pushed back his hood.
Illisius.

<207>

"Hello, Oliver," he said. Desiree walked over and stood beside him.

Oliver could barely walk anymore. He and Emalie proceeded slowly onto the disc. Oliver felt the metal beneath his feet almost as if it was pushing up against him, trying to collapse his bones, crush him. Or he was about to sink into it. He couldn't do this. Or rather, he couldn't *not* do this. There was energy here, power. He could feel the Gate vibrating his very existence.

A strange hissing sound grew behind him. Oliver turned back to see that the whole vampire crowd had moved to the edge of the disc, their numbers growing, and they were all whispering some incantation in Skrit.

Oliver found Illisius gazing at him, and smiling. As if Oliver should have been excited about this.

"We have come to end what was once begun," said Illisius, speaking loudly, as if to the entire universe. "We have come to free those who have been oppressed. We have come to make again what was imperfect."

We need Dean! Oliver shouted at Emalie.

I know.... Oliver could hear the strain in Emalie's thoughts. *I can't find him!*

"The prophecy is now complete," Illisius continued. "The Anointed will step forward and complete their destiny."

Oliver felt awash in waves of panic. This was happening too fast, and there was nothing they could do! It was terrible. The end. And the worst part was that Oliver would survive it. He was about to open the Gate and he would be fine. But as for those he loved....

He gripped Emalie's hand more tightly, and felt her shaking. *I'm so sorry*, he thought to her.

Suddenly Emalie shouted to him, *Wait!*

"We shall now—" Illisius stopped.

Oliver looked and saw that Desiree had touched Illisius's arm, and now they were looking up. There was light on their faces, but not from the Gate. This was from above.

Oliver looked up to see lights drifting down like embers from a firework, yet as they neared he could see that they were larger: luminous spheres of energy, and there seemed to be figures inside them, white-robed figures....

Mom! Emalie cried.

A scream pierced the minds of all on the plateau, the unison, demon-tinged cry of eight women. They landed in a semi-circle around the gold altar, all wielding jade mirrors in their hands.

"*Attechhhhhh!*" They cried. The Skrit for attack.

<209>

Chapter 16

THE FALLEN

Emalie let go of Oliver's hand. *Something I need to do.*

The Orani were landing, their battle cry still ringing across the plains. Oliver saw that Emalie's eyes had ignited red and searing white. *Don't worry,* Emalie thought to him. *We trained for this.*

"Desiree!" Emalie suddenly screamed aloud, yet her voice was like nothing Oliver had heard before. Actually, no, he had heard something like this before, when Emalie had been Syren. This was her inner demon unleashed. She thrust her hand out before her. A jade Architect mirror appeared in her grasp. Beams of light shot from each of the mirrors held by the Orani, all converging on Emalie's in a searing ball. Emalie lifted from the ground, her eyes burning bright red, and smiled toward Desiree, who had only just begun to thrust her hand forward, a ball of red energy forming at her fingertips.

<210>

But Emalie was first.

"Meet Eos!" she screamed. A single beam of energy, the sum of all the Orani power and that of the Architects too, burst forth from her mirror.

Desiree began to smile in a kind of defiant snarl, but the beam of light blasted into her chest and consumed her in light. She fought, staggering, then writhing.

"YOU HAVE BETRAYED YOUR BROTHERS AND SISTERS," a deep voice boomed, coming from the mirrors. The Architects speaking in unison.

Desiree's human costume began to melt away. There was a thrashing of her many arms and legs, a screech that tore at everyone's mind, and then Dead Desiree exploded in a burst of light. It was solid and blinding, and then sucked in on itself. When it was gone, no trace of the rogue Architect remained.

Emalie dropped to the ground, landing on one knee, breathing hard. The vampires had barely moved.

Illisius was just watching her, a bemused look on his face.

"Your turn," said Emalie, and she thrust her hand out again, this time firing the energy at Illisius. He casually raised his hand, meeting the burst. It slammed against his palm and sprayed in all directions. Yet despite Illisius's calm face, Oliver could see his body shuddering against the force of the Orani attack.

We can wear him down, Emalie thought to Oliver. *I think. Just need enough time.*

Maybe we can help. A new voice had arrived in their minds.

<211>

Dean! Emalie cried.

Oliver heard an uproar from the vampires. They'd barely had a chance to comprehend the arrival of the Orani and the destruction of Desiree, and now they were whirling toward some chaos behind them. Many began rushing back toward the staircase, summoning weapons into their hands.

Oliver peered over the edge of the plateau. For a moment he flinched at the sheer cliff just beyond his toes, dropping hundreds of feet to the rocky ground. He looked down toward the stairs and saw The Forsaken Legion pouring forth from the Transmitter through a curtain of red light, wielding weapons, lunging into combat with the Half-Light vampires.

Oliver spied Dean among them, near the front with Phlox and Sebastian, their battle axes whirling. Oliver didn't see Lythia, or Braiden, but the battle was raucous. For his part, Dean seemed to be doing pretty well with an axe of his own. As Oliver watched, Dean turned one vampire to ash.

Dean, get up here! Oliver heard Emalie call. She still had Illisius at bay. Now was their chance. *We need you! You're part of the Triad!*

Below, Oliver saw Dean momentarily pause. *What? I am? Really? That's kinda cool.*

Yeah, now hurry! Oliver chimed in. *Tell my parents to get you up here.*

Got it!

Oliver whirled back around. He closed his eyes and

<212>

concentrated. *Tachesss....* He summoned the rattan sticks into his hands. Ahead, Illisius was still locked against the Orani energy. Emalie still on one knee, her free hand holding the wrist of the other, aiming the blast.

Two black jets of smoke slithered onto the plateau beside him, holding Dean by each arm. He landed beside Oliver, and the smoke reformed as Phlox and Sebastian.

"Are you okay?" Phlox asked, axe raised before her.

"Yeah," said Oliver.

Dean nodded to him. "Okay, now what?"

"We join Emalie and form the Triad." Oliver nodded toward her.

"We'll cover you," said Sebastian.

Oliver started toward Emalie.

"How exactly do we form this Triad?" Dean asked, hurrying up beside him.

"Not sure." That was still a troubling question, and they had only seconds to figure it out.

"Heads up!" called Phlox. She and Sebastian whirled to face a mass of vampires racing toward them.

Oliver and Dean reached Emalie. *Emalie, I got him!* Oliver thought to her.

Okay, Emalie thought, sounding tense with the effort of aiming the light blast.

"What do you think we do now?" Dean shouted.

Um.... said Emalie. She glanced over toward her mom, who was busy feeding her energy from her Architect's mirror. She looked back, brow furrowed.

Maybe if we join hands, Oliver began—

<213>

A flash of light caught his eye. By the time he turned to Dean, whatever that light had been was gone, but Dean was clutching at his chest with his free hand. A thin trail of black smoke was curling through his fingers.

"What happened?" Oliver shouted. He scanned the melee out beyond the line of glowing Orani but couldn't see any sign of what had just occurred.

"Nnn...." said Dean, wincing, hand still at his chest. He stepped away from Oliver, half stumbling, around to the opposite side of Emalie.

"Dean, what?" Oliver shouted.

Dean shook his head back and forth. "I—No.... I won't... I...." He pulled away his hand and Oliver saw a dripping melted mass cupped in it, swirls of magenta—maybe blood?—but also silver flecks.... There was a tattered hole in his t-shirt, and through that, Oliver could see a black burn on Dean's chest.

"Cannnnnn't...." Dean moaned, but he shook the substance off his hand, gripped his axe with both hands, and began raising it with trembling arms.

Something was missing. In Dean's shirt. Wait... the Hindrian charm....

Oh no....

What? Emalie called in his mind.

"DEAN NO!" Oliver shouted.

The axe flung back high over Dean's head. Dean looked at Oliver with wide, terrified eyes. "It's Lythia! She's ordering me to—*Nooo!*" But Dean couldn't resist. The axe blade arced overhead, plummeting down with lethal speed. Toward Emalie's skull. "Oliver, STOP ME!" Dean screamed.

The truth of what was happening hit Oliver in a flash. Had to react, now! *Emalie DUCK!* he shouted and he thrust his arms, sending his rattan sticks hurtling forward, whizzing just over Emalie's head—

And impaling Dean.

The impact punched him backward. The axe swung off course, and Emalie caught a glimpse of the steel just in time to throw herself into a forward roll. The light from her hand extinguished. The axe flew free of Dean's hands and clanged off the gold floor.

Emalie sprang to a crouch and spun around. She glanced at Oliver. *I'm okay.*

Oliver just kept staring at her. He didn't want to move his eyes from her, didn't want to see what he'd done.

But Emalie looked. "Dean!" she cried and dove, landing on her knees beside him, dragging Oliver's gaze with her. Dean lay on the metal ground. One stick had caught him in the right shoulder, by his neck. The other had sunk right into the center of his chest.

"Ga—" Dean gagged and coughed. Black fluid spilled out of his mouth. He rolled weakly onto his side, and now Oliver could see both sticks protruding out of his back. And he could see the black flowing from the wounds, a pool spreading around him.

"Dean," Oliver moaned. *I had to,* he thought to Emalie.

I know, she thought back. "It's okay, Dean...."

Oliver scanned the battle. Past Phlox and Sebastian, past the Orani....

<215>

There. Crouched atop the amethyst temple: Lythia and Braiden, Lythia holding some kind of small, glowing crystal, no doubt part of the spell she'd just used to destroy Dean's protective charm.

"LYTHIA!" Oliver screamed. She'd said they were going to go to the Gate and kill the demon, but there was an easier target than the powerful Illisius. There was the demon Orani. Kill her and the prophecy ended as well. She'd planned on Dean getting close enough to do it....

Oliver couldn't believe it. He felt rage brimming inside him. After they'd worked together, after he'd finally trusted her.... If he could somehow have crossed the battle to her, Oliver felt like he would have slain Lythia with his bare hands.

But someone else had a similar feeling. "Now that wasn't very nice." Oliver turned to see Illisius standing tall in the pause in the Orani attack and brushing at his coat. He peered out toward Lythia and Braiden and raised his hand. A fireball formed around it. Illisius shook his head. "That was *mine*," he scolded. The red energy fired from his hand, searing through the air.

Lythia, her reflexes still quick, leapt from the temple. Braiden had barely moved when the fireball arrived, consuming him in a flash. Oliver cursed to himself, and hoped Illisius might throw another after her.

"Emalie!" The scream tore Oliver from his thoughts. He whirled. It was Margaret, her eyes wide, looking past Emalie.

Emalie started to spin around but Oliver saw it first.

Illisius wasn't aiming for the fleeing Lythia. Instead, he was striding forward, a column of smoke forming in his hand. He glanced at Oliver. "It's time, Oliver!" The smoke became a long, straight steel stiletto, like the one that Sebastian had used to try to kill Selene, on Mt. Morta.

"NO!" Margaret leapt to her feet, mirror igniting—

Emalie was just turning and getting to her feet when Illisius grabbed her shoulder and turned her back to him.

Oliver couldn't move, it was happening too fast, or he was too slow, or—

Illisius thrust. The stiletto plunged into Emalie's back, emerging on the other side of her heart.

"*Ahhhh!*" she screamed and the scream was in Oliver's ears and mind too and it seared white hot and made him double over and stagger.

Illisius yanked the stiletto back out. Emalie's body quivered, her eyes rolling back in her head, and she fell face-first across the center of the gold disc, her arms out, unmoving.

<217>

Chapter 17

LIGHT, DARK, CHOICE

She was just an intruder.

Just a silly human.

She'd even tried to kill him once.

But—

Quiet. Not yet....

She'd left him for two years, and never said she was sorry. Never even seemed to notice that it bothered him.

Or maybe she—

No. Wait....

She'd as much as said that they had no future together, when she pointed out how much faster she'd age. And she was right. She'd be dead, stupid human dead, before he was even old, so really who cared? What was the point?

But...

But.

She was the girl with the camera.

The splash of color in an otherwise gray world.

<218>

The hand on the back of his sweatshirt.

The secret notes beneath his desk.

Who hid in coffins, and tried strange vampire foods.

Who lit up with dangerous power.

Who sensed too much, who hurt for the loss and pain of the world.

Who helped him find the truth when no one else would.

She was the kiss goodbye.

The one who made jokes out of fairy tales.

The girl who crossed worlds with him. Faced demons.

Who died one time, to help him.

Who'd held his hand even as they marched toward their end.

Fearless.

Brave.

Emalie....

Lying still on the gold ground, the light of the Gate muted by her seeping blood.

"*NO!*" Oliver screamed.

It was too much. Emalie. Dean. His friends. Strewn across the ground. Fallen. Just like Bane....

"Emalie!" Margaret wailed. Oliver heard it like it was miles away. Out of the corner of his eye, he saw Selene grab Margaret, and strangely, the two of them winked out of sight in a flash of light. The other six Orani aimed their mirrors and fired light at Illisius directly.

He extended a hand and blocked the energy, sending it spraying harmlessly away.

Oliver just kept staring. Emalie. Dean. *No.*

<219>

Emalie.

He couldn't... anything. Think. Move. Fight. But he did tear himself from his frozen spot and fall to his knees beside her. The smell of her blood was overwhelming, like being hit with a tidal wave, crushing his senses with terrible sweetness. He shivered against it—*she would think that was awful*, he reminded himself as he so often had—and put two fingers to her neck.

Searching for her pulse...

But didn't he already know? Because normally he could hear that thumping, rushing sound, the heart pumping liquid, life, from across the room. So noisy compared to him, or anyone else he knew, that he had to fight to ignore it.

His fingers found her artery.

It was still.

"You see now, Oliver?" Illisius called to him over the clangs of battle and the humming of light. "It's all death. That's what Finity really is. A brief burst of life followed by endless death. Little candles in the eternal dark. That's all it will ever be."

Oliver lurched to his feet, stumbling back a step. *No no no no!* This was too horrible. Too terrible to have to know, to have to feel. He felt a sinking inside, his grief, already heavy from taking Jenette's, plunging lower... but he wanted even more. He couldn't feel this *enough*, wanted this pain to be as terrible and consuming as possible, like the end of the world, like relief would never come. Curse his hollow body! He needed help.

<220>

"Revelethh... lucenthh... persechhh..." he whispered.

Nathan shimmered into existence across from him, holding his own rattan sticks. He was such a small light compared to the blinding Gate, but still, even just his presence gave Oliver a meager warmth, and yet that only made the pain seep in deeper, made his gut start to quiver, his eyes squint and teeth clench.

Oliver! I was waiting for— He saw the fallen friends. *Oh no!*

Oliver looked down again. Emalie and Dean forming odd angles. No order to their arms and legs. Like some weird geometric design. He yanked his gaze toward Illisius. "YOU KILLED HER!"

"Yes," said Illisius, "but that doesn't change the fact that she would've died anyway. Just like you knew she would. Given her love for danger, probably sooner than later. But even if she had a long, full human life, what would that be... sixty more years? Seventy? Then gone forever."

"Shut up!" Oliver shouted.

"Look at her, Oliver." Illisius spoke calmly, an almost parent-like tone to his voice. "That's what *life* is. Right there. So, you can wallow in its pain and suffering... or you can end it, and be free."

Oliver did look at Emalie, but only for a moment—too much too terrible *no no no*—then at Dean—*no no no*—and thought of grabbing his fighting sticks and running at Illisius, but...

What was the point?

<221>

Not just because Illisius was so strong, standing there calmly deflecting the most powerful forces left in this fight with one hand...

But also because he was right. Wasn't he right? It all ended in death. Everything he'd come to love about the world.

Oliver, no. He's wrong, said Nathan.

Oliver just shook his head. Really, who cared if he was? It didn't even matter if Illisius was right or wrong. All this business of Finity and worlds and all of it really was nothing, nothing, *nothing* compared to the one reality, the one unchangeable truth:

Emalie was gone.

How could he go on knowing that? Why would he want to?

"You don't have to," said Illisius, reading his thoughts. "Oliver, my boy, you can choose to be free of it. Free of this world, this vampire existence, of going through your days without them." Illisius waved his free hand at Emalie and Dean. "You can be free of it. And you can free the universe of this kind of suffering forever. Not to mention freeing your own kind from prison. We can all be free of what you're feeling right now, of Finity's sickening disease. You, your parents, everyone."

Not to feel this anymore.... Illisius was right about that, too. It did feel like a sickness, something that would gnaw at his insides forever, this terrible despair. To be free of it, to just end it....

"It's your choice."

<222>

Oliver heard this, and suddenly he almost laughed. Choice.

So this, *this* was what his prophecy meant. Emalie had been brought here, had been tied to the prophecy. She was the power that no other vampire had, only her purpose was to be *killed* by Illisius. And killing her was supposed to give Oliver the power to open the Gate. To *choose* it. To choose freedom as a higher demon over this terrible suffering. As the prophecy had said, *to overcome the Architect's most powerful forces.* What were those exactly?

Whatever, it didn't matter anymore. None of it. Oliver felt a wave of exhaustion settle over him. *Emalie... Dean... I can't go on*, he thought.

And Illisius was right: he didn't have to. He could just open the Gate. Forget it. Emalie was gone. Anyone else he cared about would someday be gone too. But not his parents, his larger family, they'd exist forever with him in the new universe. That was, except for Bane.

But then was he slain for nothing? It was Nathan, asking him. *Were all of them slain for nothing?*

"That's Finity talking," said Illisius. "The idea that every life has to *mean* something. But how can they? They're not eternal. They're just a means to what's next."

Feelings, said Nathan.

What? Oliver looked over at him, his soul, the thing that made him feel good, alive, and yet... he almost didn't even want to look at Nathan anymore. Because wasn't he just another thing that Oliver could never have? Like a reminder of his emptiness? At least if he had a demon, he would have something inside. He would be complete, wouldn't he?

The thing in the prophecy, about the most powerful forces of the Architects, Nathan was saying, *I think they're feelings. Like, emotions.*

"Time to make a choice, Oliver." Illisius extended his free hand. "Take my hand and we'll begin the universe again, and end your pain forever."

The Gate suddenly burst with light, momentarily blinding them all, almost as if it had heard Illisius's request. Oliver blinked hard, and when the light cleared from his eyes, he noticed a change. Turning, he saw that the battle behind him had ended. The vampires, the Legion, Phlox and Sebastian, all were watching him. The Orani had stopped firing. Without really realizing it, Oliver had taken a step toward Illisius.

Or maybe he *had* realized it. And now everyone on the acropolis at Nexia knew that it was time for the end.

Oliver, see me clearly.

The voice of the Gate surprised him. It was loud, washing away other thoughts. Oliver shook his head, that voice was always so familiar, and always that same phrase, it had been saying that since that night in the school gym: what did it mean?

Stay out of this, Illisius said in Oliver's mind, as if replying to the Gate.

Oliver tried to look up at the Gate, but it was too blindingly bright. He turned away...

And found himself gazing at Emalie again. *Oh, Emalie.* She had been so alive, she… *She would think this was awful.* The thought struck him. How many times had he had that very thought, when he was about to do something, only to have that idea give him pause, sometimes even change his mind? The idea that *she* would think it was wrong. That he cared what she thought, that it mattered to him even in times when she wouldn't know… like now.

See me clearly, the Gate repeated.

That's enough! Illisius shouted at it.

Lying there, face down, it was true: Emalie would never know if Oliver opened the Gate. But, if she could have known, she *would* think it was awful, him ending the world, destroying all of her loved ones, all the living beings.

But, who cares? She's dead, Oliver argued back at this thought. *It doesn't matter what she thought!*

Doesn't it? asked Nathan. *It does to you.*

"It's time, Oliver!" Illisius called, his hand still extended, the clean white fingers beckoning.

Oliver tore his eyes away, back to Emalie—too horrible— to Dean. *What am I going to do without them?* he thought. *I can't go on….* His gaze landed on Nathan, the glowing light, the shape so similar to him. *I'm sorry,* said Oliver. *All of it… even you…. It all hurts too much.* Back to Emalie. *I can't…*

Oliver, no! Nathan called, extending his glowing hand toward Oliver.

Oliver turned to Illisius, the dark silhouette, also

<225>

reaching toward him. This was his choice. Nathan, the light and the pain of Finity, or Illisius, the dark and the infinite....

Wait a minute.

"Light, dark, choice," Oliver said to himself.

Illisius's face darkened, as if he'd heard this thought. "Come to me, Oliver!" His voice was edged with anger.

But Oliver felt like he'd fallen backward into an ocean. He was swimming in his head, around the hulking form of something enormous. A thought... A truth....

"Earth, eve, dawn," said Oliver. "Light, dark, choice." *Could it be?* he thought.

Nathan suddenly glowed brightly. *Yes!*

And finally, Oliver saw it.

It's me, he thought. *I am choice. I choose between the light and the dark.*

"Oliver!" Illisius took another step toward him.

Oliver looked at his demon. Time had slowed in his mind. *Eve, dawn, and then earth. Earth is the physical. In both light and dark. Me.* He glanced from Nathan to Illisius again. But there was even more: What had Dexires said, about living beings, about how the human was the highest creation of the Architects because it felt the most? Because it *was* both... and like Nathan had said, because it was both, it could *feel.*

Demon and soul. Light and dark. And choice. *Me.*

I know what the Triad of Finity is, thought Oliver.

"Come to me, Oliver!" Illisius lunged toward him. Reaching. His hand inches away.

Nathan!

<226>

Nathan raced toward him too.

Oliver knew. He knew what the Triad was. He was looking at it. He was part of it. He...

I am the Triad of Finity.

Or at least, he would be.

And though he couldn't change what had happened here tonight, what lay on the ground at his feet, he was going to save the world. *And that's what she would have wanted. And Dean, and Bane, too.*

The light, the dark and the choice. All he needed was something to bring them together.

To bind them.

And he had that, too. For taking the grief of a wraith....

Thanks, Jenette, Oliver thought.

He reached out just as Illisius arrived, grabbing the demon's wrist first. Nathan grabbed Oliver's other hand.

"*Contenethh!*" Oliver shouted.

Light burst from him.

"You can't--" Illisius began, his eyes igniting, as if he understood only now what was happening, and Oliver thought he saw fear, real fear in Illisius' eyes.

"*NO!*" the demon shouted.

Yes, said Nathan.

And in a blinding flash, Illisius and Nathan disappeared.

Oliver staggered. He felt an overwhelming surge inside him, spaces filling, flooding, pouring into every crack, warming, freezing, all at once. The light and the dark, demon and soul, both a part of him now....

And suddenly sound, and pain, movement inside him,

<227>

like everything was heaving, thumping.

"Oliver! What happened?" Phlox and Sebastian were rushing to his side. Distantly, the vampire crowd was in an uproar.

Oliver tried to speak but he couldn't. He— everything felt tight. Like he needed to—

He grabbed at his throat. *Help!* He tried to call. But nothing came out. He slapped at his mouth, at his chest, stumbling, falling backward.

Sebastian and Phlox caught him. "We have to get him out of here!" Phlox shouted.

"Over here!" It was Aunt Kathleen and the Orani.

Oliver's vision began to prickle with tiny explosions of light. Out of the corner of his eye, he saw a flash and Margaret and Selene returning. Margaret was holding a large glass jar, something glistening and silver inside, rushing to Emalie....

But Oliver lost control of his legs and arms. What was happening? He couldn't, he—

"Hold on, son," said Sebastian, catching him.

Oliver felt hands lifting him, but barely. Being carried through the crowd. It seemed to be happening to someone far away. Above, stars and worlds whirled, planets arcing, the universe intact....

Fading out.

Oliver's eyelids fluttered closed.

To black.

Chapter 18

PATIENT J-22

No one who awoke at dawn on that November Wednesday knew that they'd nearly slept through the end of the world. Life proceeded in its normal way, oblivious to the larger workings of the universe. People dreamed their dreams of little things they hoped would happen, regretted things they'd done, drank lots of coffee to shrug off that winter urge to sleep all day, and generally got on with things.

The nurses who arrived at Ballard Swedish Hospital that morning were surprised to find a patient in one of their beds. No one could locate a record of when this patient had been admitted, or who did the admitting, which caused a good amount of grumbling around the microwave in the staff kitchen.

The patient also had no identification, and so, when affixing a wrist band, a nurse identified him as J-22. J for juvenile, and twenty two for the date. The patient had no

<229>

obvious wounds, but was unconscious. He was given fluids, and put on monitors, while a search was conducted to try to discover his identity. Because of his dark clothing and the bruises all over his body, the patient was fingerprinted, and the results run against the police juvenile database. When that turned up negative, a small swab of cells was taken from the inside of the patient's cheek to run a DNA analysis.

Just after lunch, a match came in, but the hospital staff didn't believe it. The DNA matched a sample from a cold case; some detective named Pedersen had recently run DNA on hairs taken from a baby's blanket, connected to a missing child case from 1948. The hospital staff dismissed the findings. Faulty test. Because there was no way that this teen boy was Nathan Bailey, the abducted one-year-old from so long ago....

And so patient J-22 lay still on the bed, all through the day, until late afternoon, when the visitors arrived.

*   *   *

Something was booming. In the distance. Like banging on the sewer door.

Oliver heard it and thought he should get up, get out of his coffin and get ready to hide, or run, or fight. It would be Half-Light. They would be after him, no doubt having found some loophole in the prophecy. Some way to open the Gate after all....

The booming continued.

<230>

There was light, too. It was bright. The Gate? Was he still in Nexia?

Oliver slowly opened his eyes. It took some effort. They were sore, dry-feeling. That strange thumping sound was joined by clicks and beeps, and some weird movement, a quiet rushing sound, also rhythmic. Everything was cluttered, busy, like he was inside some kind of machine. And he heard a voice in the distance.

"We know him. Can't we just see him?"

Oliver's surroundings came into focus: A room with white walls. He was lying half-reclined in a bed, machines around him.

A hospital.

The windows looked out on a cloudy afternoon. Daylight. Oliver looked down and saw that his bare arms were directly in the light. He felt a surge of panic and flinched, but then noticed that his pale white skin wasn't smoking or singed. His arms looked fine. In fact, the skin wasn't exactly white...

And there was something in his arm. A tube. Sticking through the skin just above his wrist. A tube leading to a bag of some clear fluid. What was that? Some kind of force treatment?

"I'm sorry but you can't," said the husky female voice in the hall. "Only next of kin are allowed in."

"But you can't *find* any next of kin, can you?" Another voice, this one lower, almost growling. But that couldn't be—

"Listen, we're the ones who *know* him!" The first

<231>

voice. So familiar especially when angry, but no, he must have been dreaming. This was all some kind of dream. Soon he'd wake up in his coffin, or in Dr. Vincent's force resonance imager....

"You have to let us in!"

"I'm sorry," the older voice said, "we can't allow access unless we—"

There was some kind of flash of light from the hallway, like from an enchantment.

"Thanks, I knew you'd see it our way."

Footsteps.

Oliver struggled to sit up, pushing with his elbows, but there was pain, everywhere— the aching worst of all in his chest. And as he tried to move, a sucking sound, and aching pressure, like he was filling up, muscles and bones that hadn't moved for decades now having to be flexible. But why?

And that thumping.

And—

"Oh my god." Her voice was sucked up in a gasp as she entered and saw him. "Oliver!"

Oliver looked at her and felt the world momentarily wobble. Emalie.

"You—" Oliver croaked, "you're—" he tried to talk but the words hurt, his chest hurt, he had to catch his...

Breath. *I'm breathing?* He thought. His brain was spinning. *How?*

And it spun further when the figure limping along behind Emalie spoke. He was hidden in an oversized sweatshirt, the hood up. "Dude, you look terrible."

Dean. Oliver's eyes lit up. "What happened?" he whispered.

"We have *everything* to tell you!" Emalie rushed toward him, throwing herself into a chair beside the bed and grabbing his hand. Hers felt cold. But that was strange; they'd never felt cold. Emalie's hands were always warm to near-hot, because *his* were cold....

Blood makes warmth. That beating sound he kept hearing. The rhthym and the aching. Inside him....

"I was dead," said Emalie, her face getting red and puffy, tears falling. "But Mom and Selene went off after my soul. They caught it before it could escape."

Oliver remembered a glimpse of Margaret holding a large jar, something silver inside.

"And there's a time limit with that kind of thing," Emalie continued, "but they made it, and revived me and... I lived." She tapped near her sternum. "There are still bandages, and I'm sore doing pretty much anything, but Aunt Kathleen's enchantments are healing the wounds."

"Right, wounds...." Oliver looked to Dean.

"Relax, man, I'm a zombie," said Dean. "It's not like you chopped off my head. Though, you really got me good." He rubbed at his chest. "Tore me up pretty bad, and those wounds could have eventually done me in, but Phlox patched me up. And, I'm glad you did what you did."

Oliver could see Dean's smile beneath the hood. He could also see a black gash on his chin, a red sore by his

<233>

cheek, all his troubles slowly worsening, but it didn't matter. It was amazing to see him. That was all that mattered.

It's all thanks to you, Emalie thought in his head. Then she added aloud: "You did it."

Oliver nodded. He really had: formed the Triad, saved everyone. But he'd done something more than that. Something to himself. Bound a soul and demon to him…. He remembered back to Nexia. He'd been hurting. He'd fallen, blacked out. And now he was in a hospital, and there were all these sounds, of air, rhythm, and that warmth, like he was on fire inside, and that movement of air, like the world was moving through him. It had been one thing to sense the forces of the universe rushing by, but this was right there inside him, real and solid and hurting his body… Air… blood…He put a hand on his chest, felt it rising and falling. Lungs. And that rhythmic beating. Through his hand. In his ears. His neck. Pulsing as far as his toes. He… Could he possibly be? Oliver didn't even want to ask it, but he had to:

"Am I…" he croaked. "Alive?"

Emalie's tears made little rivers. She nodded enthusiastically, rubbing his arm hard, leaving momentary white streaks in the pink, pink from blood moving beneath skin…. "Yeah. You— you're alive, Oliver."

"It's crazy, dude," Dean added.

"I—" but Oliver couldn't finish. The words melted through him. *I'm alive.* He felt his heart, the burning sun inside him, speed up at the thought. He sucked in a breath

<234>

faster. Felt this weird surge of oxygen mixing in blood and tingling cells, millions of cells, tiny factories, all this movement, this burning... Life. It was a busy noisy thing like nothing he had ever imagined.

"Alive," he whispered to himself, because he was still trying to make sense of it. He'd formed the Triad. Light, dark, choice. The Triad of Finity was *life*. By binding Illisius and Nathan to himself, he had made them part of him. Demon and soul. Now he was the Triad, the pinnacle of the Architect's work.

"So, I'm like... human?"

Emalie laughed between her sobs. "Not exactly. Aunt Kathleen says you're actually something more like us, the Orani, or maybe closer to a warlock by definition."

"So you're still a freak," said Dean with a grin.

"Great," said Oliver.

Emalie continued: "Humans may have some demon fragment inside them, but not an Illisius-sized demon."

"And a soul that lived on its own for half a century," said Dean, "and a wraith's grief."

"Yeah," said Emalie, "I think it's safe to say that you're going to be a little more *supernatural* than the rest of our human high school classmates." She smiled. "Which means I *might* still let you hang out with me."

"High school?" said Oliver. "We—"

"They want to put you in a transitional home," said Emalie, "the state I mean, until they find your parents, but don't worry. We Orani can be very persuasive. Once we get you out of here, you can stay with us, at least for awhile—"

<235>

"And at my place," said Dean, "Anytime."

"And yeah," Emalie continued, "You're going to be joining the ninth grade, with me. Aunt Kathleen has friends in the enrollment office. How does that sound?"

Oliver didn't answer. Not because he didn't want to.

"Oliver?"

He wanted to say that it sounded amazing, that it was blowing his mind, that it was beyond anything he could ever have imagined, never mind last night when he was facing the end of the world, but even just lying in his coffin, day after day, knowing something was wrong with him, knowing he was hollow somehow, unfinished.

He'd been alive once. Now, he was alive again. Complete. He wanted to say how amazing that felt, how it almost felt like a *relief*, like his life was finally about to begin—which was technically true, or at least, it was about to restart after a brief sixty-six year hiatus—but...

He just suddenly found that he couldn't. Not that he couldn't find the words, but that he literally couldn't speak. His throat felt as if a ball was stuck in it, just above his windpipe. The strange, steady rhythm of air in and out was starting to hitch and halt, his eyes wincing up and all his senses seeming to cut out—

And then he felt a stinging sensation in his eyes. He coughed, choking on the ball, and suddenly, warm drops were slipping down his cheeks. His heartbeat, that loud, thumping presence in his body, so new and yet so obvious, so important, began to pick up speed. Oliver could barely comprehend what was happening. He was

<236>

too overwhelmed; the feeling was more terrifying, more desperate, and yet more exhilarating than anything he had ever known....

Oliver felt Emalie watching him. He looked up, and through his blurry eyes, saw her gazing back at him, eyes watering, lip quivering. It was as if she was a mirror, or something more—*see me clearly.... She was my gate*, he thought, *the thing that kept me on track*—and he understood now what was happening to him. It was like that night on the bluff, multiplied by a hundred. He choked up, and a small cry escaped his mouth as more tears started to fall.

Never had he imagined such a feeling.

More minutes went by, and Oliver still didn't speak, lost in the desperate, crushing feeling of crying, and this terrible-yet-wonderful synergy of being something living, a creation of light and darkness that could truly feel. His heart galloped, and he felt it slamming out against his chest, threatening to tear those long dormant muscles apart.

Oliver thought then that if he could've formed the words, he would have said that the greatest thing in the world was simply being alive.

<237>

<238>

EPILOGUE

There were many nights, as there had once been many days, when Nathan Bailey had trouble falling asleep. On some of these nights, he would sneak out alone and wander the streets. It was different, now. Though he vaguely remembered the routes he used to take, the sewers and rooftops, he knew those weren't for him anymore. When he was out, Nathan would see shadows here and there, or hear the rustle of crow's wings, the low chuckle from beneath a bridge, or the flicker of candlelight in a dark school window, and hurry along with a shiver. There were dangers in the night, things to be feared.

The night of December 28th, Nathan's fifteenth birthday, was raw and wet. They celebrated at Emalie's house, which was starting to look homey again after its long empty period. Nathan was sleeping in the basement, on a cot in the former darkroom space. It was a little bit damp and chilly, but even though Nathan now curled up in an old down comforter rather than

<239>

soil, he found that he didn't mind the cobwebs, or the nocturnal scurrying of the mice and rats.

After cake, Nathan, Emalie and Dean headed out into the dark to celebrate on their own. They rode the bus roof in silence. It was Nathan who now needed his friends to help him make the leap onto the roof, though he wasn't entirely helpless when it came to climbing around. He still had a vague sense of the forces.

What's up? Emalie asked him as they rode.

Nothing, said Nathan, but it wasn't true.

Did you like the party? She asked.

Yeah.

Did you like my present?

Nathan glanced at her and smiled. Their hands were clasped and tucked tight between their hips for warmth. *It rocks.* Emalie had gotten him a little iPod and filled it with a playlist that she'd called "Humanization." She'd also gotten him a feline's eye opal, which was used for seeing in the dark. Nathan's human eyes were pathetic at night compared to what they'd once been, though they were still superior to an average human's.

"No more listening to month-long classical music," Emalie said of the mix. "Knowing the cool bands will help you talk to the other kids."

Nathan smiled. "Right." He'd already joined the orchestra at school, blowing the music teacher's mind with his cello playing. And that had led to him making his first enemy at Roosevelt High: the principal cellist whom he'd replaced. Oh, there was a handful of lacrosse players

<240>

who seemed to have it out for him, too, but that was just because he had pale skin and was the new kid and a bunch of other clichés, and likely mostly because they were bored. Emalie was already planning some special treatment for them after the holiday vacation.

But mention of the Melancholia brought Nathan back to the initial reason for his silence on the bus ride: the birthday party had been nice. Tammy, Margaret, Cole, Mitch, they did a fine job with the cake and treats and presents, only, for the past sixty six years, Nathan had known different customs, different traditions and cake flavors…

But those weren't for the living.

He understood why they hadn't come to the hospital. Hadn't contacted him in the month since. He was alive now. A creature of the light, and, to most vampires, a lower being. And that was probably for the best, at least, that's what Nathan tried to tell himself. He wondered if he missed them, but found that he didn't know.

"Here we are," said Emalie.

The trio exited the bus in Lower Queen Anne and entered Dick's. Soon they had trays full of burgers, fries and shakes and were sitting in an orange plastic booth.

"No rats heads, I suppose," Nathan joked to Dean.

"Gross," said Emalie.

"Hrrnnn," Dean grunted in reply. There was a jangling of chains, then a snarling sniff as Dean's hooded head bent to smell the seven burgers on his plate.

"Here you go, Dean." Emalie produced a jar of

<241>

Tabasco sauce from her bag. Dean snatched it from her with a gloved hand.

Nathan and Emalie shared a look. Some nights were tough for Dean. It was normal now for him to refuse to go out in public without the hood and gloves. And he'd taken to wearing a sailor's dry suit underneath his baggy sweatshirt and jeans. It wasn't to keep water out, but to keep oozing flesh, and its odor, in.

The cravings for brains came and went, but on nights like tonight they rendered him almost mute. The chains were for everyone's safety. At home, Dean had agreed to start sleeping in a titanium cage in the basement.

They were all in danger around him. Nathan knew it would end badly someday, and yet, he was still their Dean, and he still refused to indulge in human brains and succumb completely. And even when he was in his most zombie-like state, you could still see the real him in there, now and then. The real boy that he had once been....

Having a soul only made Nathan feel more guilty, more responsible for what Dean had become. So, he had made a pledge to himself, and a pact with Emalie: They would protect him, no matter what. They would search for some way to undo his zombie condition, or at least keep it at bay. And they would always bring him along for the things he liked to do, even when he couldn't join in, at least not in a human way.

"I can't believe that Mica broke up with Dexter," Emalie said, sucking down her chocolate shake.

"Dexter's bumming," Nathan agreed.

<242>

"I tried to change her mind during Bio," said Emalie.

"Emalie's Dating Suggestion Service," Nathan joked. He'd done the lab work for both of them—he loved bio lab, particularly today, when they'd been dissecting their fetal pig again, which he was exceptionally good at—while Emalie had done a leap into Mica's head.

"But, she's dead set on it," Emalie continued. "And you know what? She hasn't told anyone this yet, but she totally has a huge crush on Parker."

Nathan smiled. "Crazy."

"Oh, hey," said Emalie, "how was gym class?"

They'd started a unit on rock climbing. The high school gym had a whole wall set up for it.

"I held back," said Nathan, "even pretended to slip once." Though he couldn't do anything like scale sheer walls or crawl across ceilings anymore, he could make easy work of a rock climbing wall. And he still had a shocking vertical leap. It was nice, especially when you were the scrawny, sun-starved new kid. "But even without trying," he added, "I still kinda set the all-time record for climbing the Expert route."

"Show off," Emalie said with a smile, but it faded as her eyes shifted to the door. "Hey look."

Nathan turned, and when he saw them, his heart jumped to a faster beat. Vampires. And one of them was Lythia. They were two steps inside when she saw the trio. Nathan just stared at her. Lythia stared back.

"Come on, girlfriend," Emalie muttered. "Just try it."

Nathan put a hand on her arm. "Not here," he said,

<243>

even though he felt a surge of rage at seeing her, "unless she tries something."

But Lythia huffed, turned to say something to her friends, and they spun and walked out. It was just as well. Someday not too long from now, Lythia would likely get her demon, and then Dean would need more protecting from her, but for the moment, she knew to stay away.

They finished their burgers, chatting about the myriad other high school dramas that were so normal to Emalie and so new to Nathan. When Dean was done, satiated and able to speak coherently again (it took five more burgers, Dean just yanking out the patties and devouring them in single bites), they headed outside.

Nathan paused on the sidewalk.

"Hey, bus stop's this way," said Emalie, tugging on his hand, but then she saw his expression and stopped. "Uh oh, there's the no-face. What's up?"

"Sorry," said Nathan. "It's just, um, I think I'm going to walk home."

"Oh." Emalie's face scrunched. "Is something—"

"Nothing," said Nathan. "It's just, you know… birthdays." He sighed. "A lot's changed since my last one. I just feel like thinking it out for a bit. You don't mind, do you?"

Emalie frowned. "Of course I mind, you jerk," she said, but then she stepped over and wrapped her arms around him. "But only 'cause I'll miss you."

Nathan kissed her. Both their lips were warm now, and Nathan felt the world slip away so there was only the feeling of Emalie, her skin, her scent, her arms. Just a kiss, no fate of the world at stake, no danger, just the two of them, finally. However good Nathan had once thought a kiss was, it was a thousand times better when you were both alive. And every one only made him ache for another. To pull Emalie closer to him, to kiss her longer, all night, until the sun rose and warmed both their faces....

"Ugh," Dean huffed after a minute.

Nathan pulled away. For now. "I'll miss you, too."

Emalie rubbed his shoulders and grinned. "Guess being alive is only going to make you more broody."

Nathan returned the grin. "Guess. See you guys tomorrow."

"Later," Dean called.

Emalie gave a little wave and turned to leave.

Nathan watched her go, then headed off alone.

He crossed streets until he reached Seattle Center. He wandered around the fountain and glanced up at the Space Needle looming high overhead, glowing in the murky fog. He remembered being up there, the fate of the Universe at stake, and swinging to safety.... The memories already seemed distant, like they were part of another existence.

He left the Center and headed up Denny Way. He was turning on Fifth Avenue when he first heard the footsteps behind him.

He kept walking, making his way over to Westlake Center. Here were more memories: the long rectangular fountain, dry in the winter, where he'd first agreed to take Emalie and Dean down into his world.

<245>

Here too was the large Christmas tree that the city put up every year. Where his life had once ended.... Nathan stopped beside it, looking up at the red and white lights, each creating a tiny halo in the fog.

The footsteps paused nearby.

"Oliver."

He turned, feeling a burst of nerves.

"Hey," he said.

Phlox and Sebastian stood together, in long coats, arms intertwined.

"Sorry," said Phlox. "Nathan."

"It's okay."

A moment of silence passed between them.

"Happy birthday," said Phlox.

"Thanks," said Nathan.

They stood there. Nathan didn't know what to say. He wondered: where had they been this last month? Or, why were they here now? And it almost made him laugh to realize that he was having that same thought he'd had with them so many times before: What were they thinking?

"We wanted to give you time," said Sebastian, as if reading his thoughts. "It must be an... adjustment."

Nathan nodded. "It's different."

Another moment passed.

"Well," said Phlox, "We wondered if you might join us. I—I made a cake."

For a moment, Nathan wondered if he should be nervous. He was a human, after all, going to a vampire's home... but he felt nothing like that. And Phlox's cake

<246>

would no doubt be delicious. "Okay," he said.

Phlox nodded. "Good. Come along, then."

Nathan walked between them. It was a long walk to Twilight Lane, and they spoke little. Just the old clicking of Phlox's heels, and the new sound of Nathan's quick breaths.

"Your grandmother and the rest of the family in Morosia were quite pleased that you saved the world," Phlox said at one point.

"Oh," said Nathan, "that's cool."

"You were very brave," Phlox added quietly. "Your father and I were quite proud."

"Thanks," Nathan mumbled, feeling a squirm of nerves at hearing this. He was pretty sure it was a good feeling.

"You seem to be getting along all right at school," Sebastian noted. "I get reports from Clarence, the janitor we have there."

"It's okay," said Nathan.

They dropped into the sewer at the base of Twilight Lane. The jump down was a little harder for Nathan than it had once been, but not too bad. As they walked up the tunnel, he noticed that the low-lit sewer didn't feel as warm to him as it used to. And yet, it smelled like it always had, damp and like candle wax, and he was glad for it.

They entered through the sewer door and headed upstairs. Nathan glanced down the hall into the crypt and could see that his coffin was gone. Only Phlox and Sebastian's remained. It made the room look big, and kind of empty.

In the kitchen, Phlox immediately moved to the counter

<247>

and pulled foil off a rectangular cake. Three plates were arranged on the kitchen island. There were heavy goblets beside two. At the place where Nathan used to sit was a Coke and a glass.

"I know it's a school night, so we can keep it brief," said Phlox, putting the cake on the table while Sebastian filled their goblets from a lead pitcher.

Nathan slid onto his usual stool. He watched as Phlox opened the fridge, its door hissing upward, revealing the hanging bags of crimson fluid, like what was inside him now, and he wondered, did his parents smell his blood? Did they sense his heart beating?

Phlox got out a bowl of whipped cream and closed the fridge.

He hadn't expected this, but sometimes Nathan had imagined being here again, and had wondered what it would feel like. He found that it felt normal, or maybe a little odd, or both.

Phlox placed the whipped cream on the table but didn't sit down. She glanced at Sebastian.

"We have something to show you, first," said Sebastian.

"Okay."

"This way." He and Phlox headed down the hallway. Nathan followed, past the living room, stopping at the door to the office.

Phlox and Sebastian had stepped inside. Nathan looked in and saw that Sebastian's antique desk was gone. In its place was a twin-sized human bed, fully made, with a crimson comforter on top. Beside it was Nathan's old

<248>

dresser, and a table with a small magmalight reading lamp.

"Do you like it?" Phlox asked quietly.

Nathan didn't know what to say. "I—" but he couldn't finish. He felt himself welling up inside.

Sebastian ruffled his hair. "It's okay. Just... something to consider. Let's go eat."

They walked back to the kitchen and sat down. Phlox served pieces of chocolate cake. "No infusions," she said of the cake, "just a raspberry sauce, and I went light on the spice."

Nathan slapped a spoonful of whipped cream on top and took a big bite. The cake was still wickedly spicey to his new human senses and he almost coughed, but he also maybe loved it. Margaret's birthday cake may have been nice, but Phlox's blew it away. "It's great," he said.

They ate quietly.

"I had quite a good time," said Phlox, after awhile, "shopping for that bed. So interesting, these human stores.... I did lots of research about coils, thread counts, all fascinating."

Nathan smiled at this.

A few more bites passed before Sebastian finally said, "We know you're mostly human now...." He was looking into the center of the table, like he was searching for words. "But you still need real parents. And as far as we're concerned, you're still our son."

Nathan took another bite of cake. A sip of Coke. He felt his insides knotting up as they had so many times at this very table, but this was different. There was a lump in

<249>

his throat. What could he say to this? How should he feel?

Except he knew how he felt.

But still…. "You guys are vampires, though," he said. "I mean, I have to sleep mostly at night, and, my food is different, and—"

"We know," said Phlox, "that things will be different. And we have no idea how to deal with a human, well, not in *this* way, anyway."

Nathan looked at her oddly. Her mouth turned slightly, and he realized that she'd just made a joke. He smiled.

"But…" Phlox's gaze turned serious again. She reached over and took his hand. And though it felt cold to him now, it was still Phlox's smooth white skin, still the slight scratch of her perfect burgundy nails. When Nathan looked up, he found her eyes glowing their wonderful turquoise. Sebastian's began to glow their fiery amber, and though Nathan didn't realize it, his living but slightly-more-than-human eyes had lit up as well, a warm crimson, as Phlox finished her thought:

"We will learn."

THE END

Begun Summer 2006
Completed Autumn 2010

<250>

ABOUT THE AUTHOR

In high school, Kevin wrote a novel in which a boy ran away from home and traveled to a land where he was separated from his inner demon, and the two had to face one another and rejoin before the boy could return home. So, in a way, Oliver Nocturne is just more of the same. Kevin wrote that book by hand in spiral notebooks, and when it wasn't finished at the end of senior year, he wrote the rest of it while manning the check-in booth at a country club, pausing every few words to sign-in guests, or to hide the notebook from his boss and coworkers. Point being, he's also always been determined to finish what he starts.

Kevin is also the author of the novel *Carlos is Gonna Get It* (Arthur A. Levine Books). His next novel, *The Lost Code: Book One of the Atlanteans* (Katherine Tegen Books), comes out in May 2012. When he's not writing books, Kevin writes songs and sings in his band *Central Services* and their kids' music counterpart *The Board of*

<251>

Education. He also teaches writing to teens at Richard Hugo House, 826 Seattle and through the Writers in the Schools program of Seattle Arts and Lectures.

Originally from Connecticut, Kevin went to Colby College in Maine and lived in Boston for awhile, where he taught elementary school science. After that, he moved to Seattle, where the moody weather and looming old school buildings inspired Oliver's story.

If you write to Kevin, he will write you back:
Email: telegramforkevin@gmail.com
Twitter: @kcemerson
Website: www.kevinemerson.net
Also: www.olivernocturne.com
You can find him on Facebook, too.

<252>